HEY YEAH RIGHT GET A LIFE

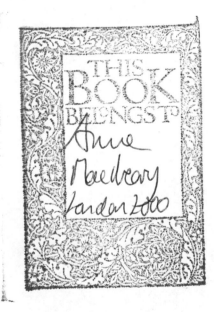

HEY YEAH RIGHT GET A LIFE

Helen Simpson

JONATHAN CAPE
LONDON

Published by Jonathan Cape 2000

2 4 6 8 10 9 7 5 3 1

Copyright © Helen Simpson 2000

Helen Simpson has asserted her right under
the Copyright, Designs and Patents Act 1988 to be identified
as the author of this work

First published in Great Britain in 2000 by Jonathan Cape
Random House, 20 Vauxhall Bridge Road, London SW1V 2SA

Random House Australia (Pty) Limited
20 Alfred Street, Milsons Point, Sydney,
New South Wales 2061, Australia

Random House New Zealand Limited
18 Poland Road, Glenfield,
Auckland 10, New Zealand

Random House (Pty) Limited
Endulini, 5A Jubilee Road, Parktown 2193, South Africa

The Random House Group Limited Reg. No. 954009

A CIP catalogue record for this book
is available from the British Library

ISBN 0-224-06082-1

Papers used by The Random House Group Limited are natural,
recyclable products made from wood grown in sustainable forests;
the manufacturing processes conform to the environmental
regulations of the country of origin

Typeset by Deltatype Limited, Birkenhead, Merseyside

Printed and bound in Great Britain by
Biddles Ltd, Guildford and King's Lynn

Contents

Some of these stories have appeared in Granta,
The New Yorker, the TLS, You Magazine,
and on Radio 3 and Radio 4

She had grown stouter and broader, so that it was hard to recognise in the robust-looking young mother the slim, mobile Natasha of old days. Her features had become more defined, and wore an expression of calm softness and serenity. Her face had no longer that ever-glowing fire of eagerness that had once constituted her chief charm. Now, often her face and body were all that was to be seen, and the soul was not visible at all.

From *War and Peace* by Leo Tolstoy,
translated by Constance Garnett

Lentils and Lilies

Jade Beaumont was technically up in her bedroom revising for the A levels which were now only weeks away. Her school gave them study days at home, after lectures on trust and idleness. She was supposed to be sorting out the differences between Wordsworth and Coleridge at the moment.

Down along the suburban pleasantness of Miniver Road the pavements were shaded by fruit trees, and the front gardens of the little Edwardian villas smiled back at her with early lilac, bushes of crimson flowering currant and the myopic blue dazzle of forget-me-nots. She felt light on her feet and clever, like a cat, snuffing the air, pinching a pungent currant leaf.

There was a belief held by Jade's set that the earlier you hardened yourself off and bared your skin, the more lasting the eventual tan; and so she had that morning pulled on a brief white skirt and T-shirt. She was on her way to an interview for a holiday job at the garden centre. Summer! She couldn't wait. The morning was fair but chilly and the white-gold hairs on her arms and legs stood up and curved to form an invisible reticulation, trapping a layer of warm air a good centimetre deep.

1

I may not hope from outward forms to win
The passion and the life, whose fountains are within.

That was cool, but Coleridge was a minefield. Just when
you thought he'd said something really brilliant, he went
raving off full steam ahead into nothingness. He was a
nightmare to write about. Anyway, she herself found
outward forms utterly absorbing, the colour of clothes, the
texture of skin, the smell of food and flowers. She couldn't
see the point of extrapolation. Keats was obviously so
much better than the others, but you didn't get the choice
of questions with him.

She paused to inhale the sweet air around a philadel-
phus Belle Etoile, then noticed the host of tired daffodils at
its feet.

> Shades of the prison-house begin to close
> Upon the growing boy,
> But he beholds the light, and whence it flows,
> He sees it in his joy.

She looked back down her years at school, the reined-in
feeling, the stupors of boredom, the teachers in the
classrooms like tired lion-tamers, and felt quite the opposite. She was about to be let out. And every day when she
left the house, there was the excitement of being noticed,
the warmth of eye-beams, the unfolding consciousness of
her own attractive powers. She was the focus of every film
she saw, every novel she read. She was about to start
careering round like a lustrous loose cannon.

Full soon thy soul shall have her earthly freight,

And custom lie upon thee with a weight,
Heavy as frost, and deep almost as life!

She was never going to go dead inside or live somewhere boring like this, and she would make sure she was in charge at any work she did and not let it run her. She would never be like her mother, making rotas and lists and endless arrangements, lost forever in a forest of twitching detail with her tense talk of juggling and her self-importance about her precious job and her joyless 'running the family'. No, life was not some sort of military campaign; or, at least, *hers* would not be.

When she thought of her mother, she saw tendons and hawsers, a taut figure at the front door screaming at them all to do their music practice. She was always off out; she made them do what she said by remote control. Her trouble was, she'd forgotten how to relax. It was no wonder Dad was like he was.

And everybody said she was so amazing, what she managed to pack into twenty-four hours. Dad worked hard, they said, but she worked hard too *and* did the home shift, whatever that was. Not really so very amazing though; she'd forgotten to get petrol a couple of weeks ago, and the school run had ground to a halt. In fact some people might say downright inefficient.

On the opposite side of the road, a tall girl trailed past with a double buggy of grizzling babies, a Walkman's shrunken tinkling at her ears. Au pair, remarked Jade expertly to herself, scrutinising the girl's shoes, cerise plastic jellies set with glitter. She wanted some just like that, but without the purple edging.

She herself had been dragged up by a string of au pairs.

3

Her mother hated it when she said that. After all, she *was* supposed to take delight in us! thought Jade viciously, standing stock-still, outraged; like, *be* there with us. For us. Fair seed-time had my soul I *don't* think.

Above her the cherry trees were fleecy and packed with a foam of white petals. Light warm rays of the sun reached her upturned face like kisses, refracted as a fizzy dazzle through the fringing of her eyelashes. She turned to the garden beside her and stared straight into a magnolia tree, the skin of its flowers' stiff curves streaked with a sexual crimson. She was transported by the light and the trees, and just as her child self had once played the miniature warrior heroine down green alleys, so she saw her self now floating in this soft sunshine, moving like a panther into the long jewelled narrative which was her future.

Choice landscapes and triumphs and adventures quivered, quaintly framed there in the zigzag light like pendant crystals on a chandelier. There was the asterisk trail of a shooting star, on and on for years until it petered out at about thirty-three or thirty-four, leaving her at some point of self-apotheosis, high and nobly invulnerable, one of Tiepolo's ceiling princesses looking down in beautiful amusement from a movie-star cloud. This was about as far as any of the novels and films took her too.

A pleasurable sigh escaped her as the vision faded, and she started walking again, on past the tranquil houses, the coloured glass in a hall window staining the domestic light, a child's bicycle propped against the trunk of a standard rose. She sensed babies breathing in cots in upstairs rooms, and solitary women becalmed somewhere downstairs, chopping fruit or on the telephone organising some toddler tea. It really was suburban purdah round here. They were like battery hens, weren't they, rows of identical hutches, so neat and tidy and narrow-minded. Imagine staying in all day, stewing in your own juices. Weren't they bored out of their skulls? It was beyond her comprehension.

And so materialistic, she scoffed, observing the pelmetted strawberry-thief curtains framing a front room window; so bourgeois. Whereas her gap-year cousin had just been all over India for under £200.

> The world is too much with us; late and soon,
> Getting and spending, we lay waste our powers.
> Little we see in Nature that is ours;
> We have given our hearts away, a sordid boon!

Although after a good patch of freedom she fully intended to pursue a successful career, the way ahead paved by her future degrees in Business Studies and Marketing. But she would never end up anywhere like here. No! It would be a converted warehouse with semi-astral views and no furniture. Except perhaps for the ultimate sofa.

Jade rounded the corner into the next road, and suddenly there on the pavement ahead of her was trouble. A child was lying flat down on its back screaming while a man in a boilersuit crouched over it, his anti-dust mask lifted to his forehead like a frogman. Above them both stood a broad fair woman, urgently advising the child to calm down.

'You'll be better with a child than I am,' said the workman gratefully as Jade approached, and before she could agree – or disagree – he had shot off back to his sand-blasting.

'She's stuck a lentil up her nose,' said the woman crossly, worriedly. 'She's done it before. More than once. I've got to get it out.'

She waved a pair of eyebrow tweezers in the air. Jade glanced down at the chubby blubbering child, her small squat nose and mess of tears and mucus, and moved away uneasily.

'We're always down at Casualty,' said the mother, as rapidly desperate as a talentless stand-up comedian. 'Last week she swallowed a penny. Casualty said, a penny's OK, wait for it to come out the other end. Which it did. But they'd have had to open her up if it had been a five-pence piece, something to do with the serration or the size. Then she pushed a drawing pin up her nose. They were worried it might get into her brain. But she sneezed it out. One time she even pushed a chip up her nostril, really far, and it needed extracting from the sinus tubes.'

Jade gasped fastidiously and stepped back.

'Maybe we should get her indoors,' suggested the woman, her hand on Jade's arm. 'It's that house there across the road.'

'I don't think . . .' started Jade.

'The baby, oh the baby!' yelped the woman. 'He's in the car. I forgot. I'll have to . . .'

Before Jade could escape, the woman was running like an ostrich across the road towards a blue Volvo, its passenger door open onto the pavement, where from inside came the sobbing of the strapped-in baby. Jade tutted, glancing down at her immaculate clothes, but she had no option really but to pick up the wailing child and follow the mother. She did not want to be implicated in the flabby womany-ness of the proceedings, and stared crossly at this overweight figure ahead of her, ludicrously top-heavy in its bulky stained sweatshirt and sagging leggings.

Closer up, in the hallway, her hyperaesthetic teenage eyes observed the mother's ragged cuticles, the graceless way her heels stuck out from the backs of her sandals like hunks of Parmesan, and the eyes which had dwindled to dull pinheads. The baby in her arms was dark red as a crab apple from bellowing, but calmed down when a bottle was plugged into its mouth.

It was worse in the front room. Jade lowered her snuffling burden to the carpet and looked around her with undisguised disdain. The furniture was all boring and ugly while the pictures, well the pictures were like a propaganda campaign for family values – endless groupings on walls and ledges and shelves of wedding pictures and baby photos, a fluttery white suffocation of clichés.

The coffee table held a flashing ansaphone and a hideous orange Amaryllis lily on its last legs, red-gold anthers shedding pollen. Jade sat down beside it and traced her initials in this yolk-yellow dust with her fingertip.

'I used to love gardening,' said the woman, seeing this. 'But there's no time now. I've got an Apple up in the spare room, I try to keep a bit of part-time going during their naps. Freelance PR. Typing CVs.'

She waved the tweezers again and knelt above her daughter on the carpet.

I wouldn't let you loose on my CV, thought Jade, recoiling. Not in a million years. It'd come back with jam all over it.

The little girl was quite a solid child and tried to control her crying, allowing herself to be comforted in between the probings inside her face. But she was growing hotter, and when, at the woman's request, Jade unwillingly held her, she was like a small combustion engine, full of distress.

'See, if I hold her down, you have a try,' said the woman, handing her the tweezers.

Jade was appalled and fascinated. She peered up the child's nose and could see a grey-green disc at the top of one fleshy nostril. Tentatively she waved the silver tongs. Sensibly the child began to howl. The mother clamped her head and shoulders down with tired violence.

'I don't think I'd better do this,' said Jade. She was frightened that metal inside the warm young face combined with sudden fierce movement could be a disastrous combination.

The woman tried again and the walls rang with her daughter's screams.

'Oh God,' she said. 'What can I do?'

'Ring your husband?' suggested Jade.

'He's in Leeds,' said the woman. 'Or is it Manchester. Oh dear.'

'Ha,' said Jade. You'd think it was the fifties, men roaming the world while the women stayed indoors. The personal was the political, hadn't she heard?

'I've got to make a phone call to say I'll be late,' said the woman, distracted yet listless. She seemed unable to think beyond the next few minutes or to formulate a plan of action, as though in a state of terminal exhaustion. Jade felt obscurely resentful. If she ever found herself in this sort of situation, a man, babies, etcetera; when the time came; IF. Well, he would be responsible for half the childcare and half the housework. At least. She believed in justice, unlike this useless great lump.

'Why don't you ring Casualty?' she suggested. 'See what the queues are like?'

'I did that before,' said the woman dully. 'They said, try to get it out yourself.'

'I'm sorry,' said Jade, standing up. 'I'm on my way to an interview. I'll be late if I stay.' People should deal with their own problems, she wanted to say; you shouldn't get yourself into situations you can't handle then slop all over everybody else.

'Yes,' said the woman. 'Thank you anyway.'

'You could ring the doctor,' said Jade on the way to the front door. 'Ask for an emergency appointment.'

'I'll do that next,' said the woman, brightening a little; then added suddenly, 'This year has been the hardest of my life. The two of them.'

'My mother's got four,' said Jade censoriously. '*And* a job. Goodbye.'

She turned with relief back into the shining spring morning and started to sprint, fast and light, as quick off the blocks as Atalanta.

Café Society

Two shattered women and a bright-eyed child have just sat down at the window table in the café. Both women hope to talk, for their minds to meet; at the same time they are aware that the odds against this happening are about fifty to one. Still, they have decided to back that dark horse Intimacy, somewhere out there muffledly galloping. They order coffee, and toast for the boy, who seizes a teaspoon and starts to bash away at the cracked ice marbling of the formica table.

'No, Ben,' says his mother, prising the spoon from his fingers and diverting his attention to the basket of sugar sachets. She flings discreet glances at the surrounding tables, gauging the degrees of irritability of those nearest. There are several other places they could have chosen, but this sandwich bar is where they came.

They might have gone to McDonald's, so cheap and tolerant, packed with flat light and fat smells and unofficial crêche clamour. There they could have slumped like the old punchbags they are while Ben screeched and flew around with the other children. McDonald's is essentially a wordless experience, though, and they both want to see if they can for a wonder exchange some words. Then there is

Pete's Café on the main road, a lovely steamy unbuttoned room where men sit in their work clothes in a friendly fug of bonhomie and banter, smoking, stirring silver streams of sugar into mugs of bright brown tea. But it would not be fair to take this child in there and spoil that Edenic all-day-breakfast fun. It would take the insensitivity of an ox. Unthinkable.

Here is all right. They get all sorts here. Here is used to women walking in with that look on their faces – 'What hit me?' Even now there is a confused-looking specimen up there ordering a decaffitated coffee, takeaway, at the counter.

'Every now and then I think *I* might give it up, see if that helps,' says Frances. 'Caffeine. But then I reckon it's just a drop in the ocean.'

Ben rocks backwards in his chair a few times, seeing how far he can go. He is making a resonant zooming noise behind his teeth, but not very loudly yet. Sally keeps her baggy eye on him and says, 'Sometimes I think I'm just pathetic but then other times I think, I'm not a tank.'

'Cannonfodder,' observes Frances.

'It's all right if you're the sort who can manage on four hours,' says Sally. 'Churchill. Thatcher. Bugger.'

Ben, having tipped his chair to the point of no return, carries on down towards the floor in slow motion. Frances dives in and with quiet skill prevents infant skull from hitting lino-clad concrete.

'Reflexes,' says Sally gratefully. 'Shot to pieces.'

She clasps the shaken child to her coat with absent fervour. He is drawing breath for a blare of delayed shock when the arrival of the toast deflects him.

'The camel's back,' says Sally obscurely.

'Not funny,' comments Frances, who understands that she is referring to sleep, or its absence.

Ben takes the buttery knife from the side of his plate and waves it in the air, then drops it onto his mother's coat sleeve. From there it falls to her lap and then, noisily, to the floor. She dabs at the butter stains with a tissue and bangs her forehead as she reaches beneath the table for the knife. Ben laughs and sandpapers his chin with a square of toast.

This woman Sally has a drinker's face, but her lustreless grey skin and saurian eye come not from alcohol but from prolonged lack of sleep.

As a former research student it has often occurred to her that a medical or sociology post-graduate might profitably study the phenomenon in society of a large number of professional women in their thirties suffering from exhaustion. Her third child, this bouncing boy, has woken at least four times a night since he was born. Most mornings he won't go back to sleep after five, so she has him in with her jumping and playing and singing. She hasn't shared a bedroom with her husband for eighteen months now. She'd carried on full-time through the first and second. They *slept. Luck of the draw. Yes of course she has talked to her health visitor about this, she has taken the boy to a sleep clinic, she has rung Cry-sis and listened to unseen mothers in the same foundering boat. The health visitor booked her into a sleep counselling course which involved her taking an afternoon every week off work, driving an hour's round trip on the North Circular, only to listen to some well-meaning woman tell her what damage this sleep pattern was causing to the family unit, to her health, to her marriage, to the boy's less demanding siblings. Well she knew all that anyway, didn't she? After the third session she said, what's the point? Not every problem has a solution, she decided, and here it is obviously a*

*brutally simple question of survival, of whether she cracks before he
starts sleeping through. It's years now.*

These thoughts flash through her mind, vivid and open,
but must remain unspoken as Ben's presence precludes
anything much in the way of communication beyond
blinking in Morse. The few words she has exchanged with
this woman Frances, known only by sight after all from the
nursery school queue, are the merest tips of icebergs. Such
thoughts are dangerous to articulate anyway, bringing up
into the air what has been submerged. Nearly all faces
close in censorship at the merest hint of such talk. Put up
and shut up is the rule, except with fellow mothers. Even
then it can be taken as letting the side down. She yawns
uncontrollably so that her eyes water, leaving her with the
face of a bloodhound.

From her handbag this tired woman Sally takes a pad
and felt tips and places them in front of her son Ben, who is
rolling his eyes and braying like a donkey.

'Shush Ben,' she says. 'You're not a donkey.'

He looks at her with beautiful affectless eyes. He sucks in
air and starts up a series of guttural snorts.

'You're not a piggy, Ben, stop it,' says Sally.

'Piggy,' says Ben, laughing with lunatic fervour.

'They were brilliant at work, they bent over backwards,'
says Sally, rapidly, anyway. 'It was me that resigned, I
thought it wasn't fair on them. I was going into work for a
rest. Ben!'

'That's hard,' says Frances, watching as Sally straightens
the boy in his chair and tries to engage him in colouring a
picture of a rabbit in police uniform.

'Do you work then?' asks Sally, filling in one long furry ear with pink.

'Yes. No,' says Frances. 'I shouldn't be here! You know, round the edges at the moment. I mean, I must. I have. Always. Unthinkable! But, erm. You know. Freelance at the moment.'

Ben pushes the paper away from him and grasps at a handful of felt tips. He throws them against the window and cheers at the clatter they make on impact.

'No, Ben!' growls Sally through clenched teeth. 'Naughty.'

The two women grovel under the table picking up pens. Ben throws a few more after them.

What Frances would have said had there been a quiet patch of more than five seconds, was, that she had worked full-time all through the babyhood of her first child, Emma, and also until her second, Rose, was three, as well as running the domestic circus, functioning as the beating heart of the family while deferring to the demands of her partner's job in that it was always her rather than him who took a day off sick when one of the girls sprained a wrist or starred in a concert, and her too of course who was responsible for finding, organising and paying for childcare and for the necessary expenditure of countless megavolts of the vicarious emotional and practical energy involved in having someone else look after your babies while you are outside the house all day, all the deeply unrestful habits of vigilance masquerading as 'every confidence' in the nanny who would, perfectly reasonably, really rather be an aerobics instructor working on Legs Tums 'n Bums.

Then there was one nanny-based strappado too many; and she cracked. After all those years. She had come home unexpectedly in the afternoon to find the woman fast asleep on the sofa, clubbed out as she later put it, while Emma and Rose played on the stairs with needles and matches or some such. Could be worse, her sensible woman-in-the-workplace voice said; she's young, she likes a good time and why shouldn't she; nothing happened, *did it? To hell with that, her mother-in-the-house voice said; I could be the one on the sofa rather than out there busting a gut and barely breaking even.*

The nanny before had been a secret smacker, the knowledge of which made Frances moan aloud in the small hours (and, if she but knew it, would do so until she died).

She needed work, she loved work, she was educated for it. Didn't she, Sally, feel the same way? She'd never asked her partner for money; no, they were equals, pulling together. Well, work was fabulous while you were there, it was what you had to do before and after work that was the killer. It was good for the girls to see their mother out working in the real world, he *said when* she *talked of feeling torn apart; a role model. There's no need to feel guilty, he would begin, with God-like compassion. It's not guilt, you fool. It's the unwelcome awareness that being daily ripped in half is not good, not even ultimately. I agree with all the reasons. 'I'm sorry, they've got to realise that you are a person in your own right and have work to do.' I couldn't agree more. 'Women have always worked, except for that brief sinister time in the fifties.' Yes. But had they always had to work a ten-hour day at a full hour's commuting distance from their babies while not showing by a murmur or a flicker what this was doing to them?*

So here she was after all these years 'gone freelance', that coy phrase, cramming a full-time job into their school hours and also the evenings once they'd gone to bed. She had a large envelope of sweets pinned to the wall by the telephone so that she could receive work calls to the noise of lollipop-sucking rather than shrilling and howls. And now, of course, she had no sick pay, paid holiday,

*pension or maternity leave should she be so foolish as to find herself
pregnant again. Just as the Welfare State she'd been raised to lean
on was packing up.*

Unfortunately not one word of this makes it into the light
of day, as Ben is creating.

'It was more fun at work,' Frances bursts out, watching
Sally wipe the child's buttery jawline with another of the
inexhaustible supply of tissues from her bag. 'You get some
respect at work.'

'My last childminder,' says Sally. She flinches.

'Snap,' says Frances.

The two women sip their powerless cappuccinos.

'In a couple of years' time, when this one starts school,'
says Sally, 'I could probably get back, get by with an au
pair in term-time. Someone to collect them from school,
get their tea. But then there's the holidays.'

'Very long, the holidays,' agrees Frances.

'Not fair on the poor girl,' says Sally. 'Not when she
doesn't speak English. Now if it was just Leo he'd be fine,'
she continues, off on another tack, thinking aloud about
her two eldest children. 'But Gemma is different.'

The child Ben slides off his chair and runs over to the
glass-fronted display of sandwich fillings, the metal trays of
damp cheese, dead ham and tired old tuna mixed with
sweetcorn kernels. He starts to hit the glass with the flat of
his hand. There is a collective intake of breath and
everyone turns to stare. As she lurches over to apologise
and expostulate, Sally's mind continues to follow her train
of thought, silently addressing Frances even if all that
Frances can see of her is a bumbling, clucking blur.

Children are all different, Sally thinks on, and they are different from birth. Her own son Leo has a robust nature, a level temperament and the valuable ability to amuse himself, which is what makes him so easy to care for. He has smilingly greeted more than half a dozen nannies and childminders in his time, and waved them goodbye with equal cheeriness. Gemma, however, was born more anxious, less spirited. She cries easily and when her mother used to leave the house for work would abandon herself to despair. She is crushingly jealous of this youngest child Ben. She wants to sit on Sally's lap all the time when she is there, and nags and whines like a neglected wife, and clings so hard that all around are uncomfortably filled with irritation. She has formed fervid attachments to the aforementioned nannies, and has wept bitterly at their various departures. Well, Gemma may thrive better now her mother is at home, or she may not; the same could be said of her mother. Time will tell, but by then of course it will be then and not now, and Sally will be unemployable whichever way it has turned out.

'Oof,' grunts Sally, returning with her son, who leaps within her arms like a young dolphin. She sits him firmly on his chair again.

'My neighbour's nanny wrote their car off last week,' says Frances. 'Nobody hurt, luckily.'

They both shudder.

'We're so lucky,' they agree, po-faced, glum, gazing at zany Ben as he stabs holes into the police rabbit with a sharp red pen. Sally yawns uncontrollably, then Frances starts up where she leaves off.

After all, they're getting nowhere fast.

An elderly woman pauses as she edges past their table on the way to the till. She cocks her head on one side and smiles brightly at Ben, whose mouth drops open. He stares at her, transfixed, with the expression of a seraph who has understood the mystery of the sixth pair of wings. Sally knows that he is in fact temporarily dumbstruck by the woman's tremendous wart, which sits at the corner of her mouth with several black hairs sprouting from it.

'What a handsome little fellow,' says the woman fondly. 'Make the most of it, dear,' she continues, smiling at Sally. 'It goes so fast.' Sally tenses as she smiles brightly back, willing her son not to produce one of his devastating monosyllables. Surely he does not know the word for wart yet.

'Such a short time,' repeats the woman, damp-eyed.

Well, not really, thinks Frances. Sometimes it takes an hour to go a hundred yards. Now she knows what she knows she puts it at three and a half years per child, the time spent exhausted, absorbed, used up; and, what's more, if not, then something's wrong. That's a whole decade if you have three! This is accurate, wouldn't you agree, she wants to ask Sally; this is surely true for all but those women with Olympic physical stamina, cast-iron immune systems, steel-clad nerves and sensitivities. Extraordinary women; heroines, in fact. But what about the strugglers? The ordinary mother strugglers? Why do they educate us, Sally, only to make it so hard for us to work afterwards? Why don't they insist on hysterectomies for girls who want further education and have done with it? Of course none of this will get said. There is simply no airspace.

Ben's eyes have sharpened and focused on his admirer's huge side-of-the-mouth wart.

'Witch,' he says, loud and distinct.

'Ben,' says Sally. She looks ready to cry, and so does the

older woman, who smiles with a hurt face and says, 'Don't worry, dear, he didn't mean anything,' and moves off.

'WITCH', shouts Ben, following her with his eyes.

At this point, Sally and Frances give up. With a scraping of chairs and a flailing of coats, they wordlessly heave themselves and Ben and his paraphernalia up to the counter, and pay, and go. They won't try that again in a hurry. They smile briefly at each other as they say goodbye, wry and guarded. They have exchanged little more than two hundred words inside this hour, and how much friendship can you base on that?

After all, it's important to put up a decent apologia for your life; well, it is to other people, mostly; to come up with a convincing defence, to argue your corner. It's nothing but healthy, the way the sanguine mind does leap around looking for the advantages of any new shift in situation. And if you can't, or won't, you will be shunned. You will appear to be a whiner, or a malcontent. Frances knows this, and so does Sally.

Even so they pause and turn and give each other a brief, gruff, foolish hug, with the child safely sandwiched between them.

Hey Yeah Right Get a Life

Dorrie stood at the edge of the early morning garden and inhaled a column of chilly air. After the mulch of soft sheets and stumbling down through the domestic rubble and crumbs and sleeping bodies, it made her gasp with delight, outside, the rough half-light of March and its menthol coldness.

The only other creature apart from herself was next door's cat which sauntered the length of the fence's top edge stately as a *fin de siècle* roué returning from a night of pleasure. That was what she was after, the old feline assurance that she had a place here. Of course you couldn't expect to remain inviolate; but surely there had to be some part of yourself you could call your own without causing trouble. It couldn't *all* be spoken for. She watched the cat hunch its shoulders and soundlessly pour itself from the fence onto the path.

Nowadays those few who continued to see Dorrie at all registered her as a gloomy, timid woman who had grown rather fat and over-protective of her three infants. They sighed with impatient pity to observe how easily small anxieties took possession of her, how her sense of proportion appeared to have receded along with her horizons.

She was never still, she was always available, a conciliatory twittering fusspot. Since the arrival of the children, one, two and then three, in the space of four years, she had broken herself into little pieces like a biscuit and was now scattered all over the place. The urge – indeed, the necessity – to give everything, to throw herself on the bonfire, had been shocking; but now it was starting to wear off.

Back in the warmth of her side of the bed she lay listening to Max's breathing, and the clink and wheezing protest of a milk float, then the first front doors slamming as the trainee accountants and solicitors set off for the station. There was a light pattering across the carpet and a small round figure stood by the bed. She could see the gleam of his eyes and teeth smiling conspiratorially in the blanching dark.

'Come on then,' she whispered. 'Don't wake Daddy.'

He climbed into bed and curled into her, his head on her shoulder, his face a few inches from hers, gazed into her eyes and heaved a happy sigh. They lay looking at each other, breathing in each other's sleepy scent; his eyes were guileless, unguarded and intent, and he gave a little occasional beatific smile.

'Where's your pyjama top?' she whispered.

'Took it *off*,' he whispered back. 'Too itchy.'

'It's *not* itchy,' she tutted. 'I'll put some special oil in your bath tonight.'

His chest was like a huge warm baroque pearl. She satined the side of her face against it for a moment.

'When are you going to stop wearing nappies at night?' she scolded in a whisper.

'When I'm four,' he chuckled, and shifted his pumpkin padding squarely onto her lap.

Max stirred and muttered something.

'Ssssh,' said Robin, placing a forefinger against his mother's lips and widening his eyes for emphasis.

They watched Max's dark bearded face break into a yawn, a seadog or a seagod about to rally his crew. He was waking up. Robin wriggled under the bedclothes to hide. Last night it had been her under the bedclothes and Max's hands on her head while she brought him off with her mouth. Then she had curled into him, her head on his shoulder, until he fell into a dense sleep, and she basked like a lioness in the sun. Next, gently unwinding herself from his knotty embrace she had glided along to the next room and plucked this heavy boy from his bed, standing him, sleep-dazed, in front of the lavatory, pointing the shrimp of his penis for him, whispering encouragement as the water hissed, before closing in on him with the midnight nappy.

Max's eyes flickered awake and he smiled at Dorrie.

'Mmmm,' he said. 'Come here.' He reached over and grabbed her, buried his face in her neck, and then as he reached downwards his hands encountered his son.

'No! No!' screeched Robin, laughing hectically. 'Get *away*, Daddy!'

This brought his siblings, Martin and Maxine, running from their bedroom and they hurled themselves into the heap of bodies. Max struggled out of it growling, and was gone.

The three children shoved and biffed their way into shares of her supine body. Robin clung to his central stake, arms round her neck, head between her breasts, kicking out at attempts to supplant him. Martin hooked his legs round her waist and lay under her left arm gnawing his nails and complaining it wasn't fair. Maxine burrowed at her right side, all elbows and knees, until she settled in the crook of her other arm, her head beside Dorrie's on the pillow.

'Mummy. A good heart is never proud. Is that true?' said Maxine.

'What?'

'It was on my *Little Mermaid* tape. I can make my eyes squelch, listen.'

'Oof, careful, Robin,' said Dorrie, as Robin brought his head up under her chin and crashed her teeth together.

'Goodbye,' said Max from the doorway.

'Don't forget we're going out tonight,' said Dorrie from the pillows.

'Oh yes,' said Max. He looked at the heap of bodies on the bed. 'Your mother and I were married eight years ago today,' he said into the air, piously.

'Where was *I*?' said Maxine.

'*Not* going out,' hissed Robin, gripping Dorrie more tightly. 'Stay inner house, Mummy.'

'And I'm not going to stand for any nonsense like that,' growled Max. He glared at his youngest son. 'Get off your mother, she can't move. It's ridiculous.'

'It's all right, Max,' said Dorrie. 'Don't make yourself late.'

'Go away, Daddy,' shouted Robin.

'Yeah,' joined in Martin and Maxine. 'Go away, Daddy.'

Max glared at them impotently, then turned on his heel

like a pantomime villain. A moment later they heard the front door slam.

'Yesss!' said Robin, punching the air with his dimpled fist. The bed heaved with cheers and chuckles.

'You shouldn't talk to Daddy like that,' said Dorrie.

'Horble Daddy,' said Robin dismissively.

'He's not horble,' huffed Dorrie. 'Horrible. Time to get up.'

They all squealed and clutched her harder, staking her down with sharp elbows and knees wherever they could.

'You're hurting me,' complained Dorrie. 'Come on, it really is time to get up.' And at last she extracted herself like a slow giantess from the cluster of children, gently detaching their fingers from her limbs and nightdress.

When she turned back from drawing the curtains, Martin was painting his shins with a stick of deodorant while Maxine sat on the floor, galloping her round bare heels in the cups of a discarded bra, pulling on the straps like a jockey, with shouts of 'Ya! Ya! Giddy up boy!' Robin ran round and round his mother's legs, wrapping and rewrapping her nightdress. Then he rolled on the carpet with both hands round her ankle, a lively leg-iron, singing alleluia, alleluia, alleluia.

'Don't do that, Martin,' said Dorrie as she climbed into yesterday's jeans and sweatshirt. But he was already on to something else, crossing the floor with a bow-legged rocking gait, a pillow across his shoulders, groaning under its imaginary weight and bulk.

'I'm Robin Hood carrying a deer,' he grinned back over his shoulder. Maxine roared with laughter, hearty as a Tudor despot.

'Come on, darlings,' Dorrie expostulated feebly. 'Help me get you dressed.'

They ran around her and across the landing, ignoring her, screeching, singing, bellowing insults and roaring into the stairwell. She pulled vests and socks and jumpers from various drawers, stepping around them like a slave during a palace orgy. Their separate energies whizzed through the air, colliding constantly, as random as the weather. She grabbed Martin as he shot past and started to strip off his nightclothes.

'No!' he yelled and tore himself free, running off trouserless. He was as quick as she was slow. It was like wading through mud after dragonflies.

'I hate you!' he was screaming at Maxine now for some reason. 'I wish you were dead!'

'Now now,' said Dorrie. 'That's not very nice, is it.'

Then there were pinches and thumps and full-chested bellows of rage. By the time she had herded them down for the cornflakes stage, they had lived through as many variants of passion as occur in the average Shakespeare play. She looked at their momentarily woebegone faces streaked with tears of fury over whichever was the most recent hair-pulling or jealousy or bruising, she had lost track, and said with deliberate cheer, 'Goodness, if we could save all the tears from getting ready in the mornings, if we could collect them in a bucket, I could use them to do the washing up.'

All three faces broke into wreathed smiles and appreciative laughter at this sally, and then the row started up again. They did not take turns to talk, but cut across each other's words with reckless thoughtlessness. She was trying to think through the hairbrushing, shoe-hunting, tooth-cleaning, packed lunch for Martin, empty toilet roll cylinder for Maxine's Miss Atkinson, with an eye on the clock, but it was a non-starter.

'SHUSH,' she shouted. 'I can't hear myself THINK.'

'Are you thinking?' asked Maxine curiously.

'No,' she said. 'Hurry UP.'

It was not in fact possible to think under these conditions; no train of thought could ever quite leave the platform, let alone arrive at any sort of destination. This was what the mothers at the school gates meant when they said they were brain-dead, when they told the joke about the secret of childcare being a frontal lobotomy or a bottle in front of me. This was why she had started waking in the small hours, she realised, even though heaven knew she was tired enough without that, even though she was still being woken once or twice a night by one or the other of them; not Max because he had to be fresh for work and anyway they wouldn't want him. They wanted *her*. But when they were all safe, breathing regularly, asleep, quiet, she was able at last to wait for herself to grow still, to grow still and alive so that the sediment settled and things grew clearer. So that she could *think*.

'Mrs Piper said Jonathan had nits and she sent him home,' said Martin, lifting his face up. She was brushing his hair, and pushed his brow back down against her breastbone. Then, more muffled, came, '*Don't* make me look like Elvis de Presto.'

'What I want to know, Mum,' he said as she pushed him back and knelt at Maxine's feet to struggle with her shoe buckles. 'What I *need* to know, nobody will tell me,' he continued crossly, 'is, is God there, *can* he hold the whole world in his hand – or is he like the Borrowers? I mean, what is he? Is he a man? Is he a cow?'

She was working grimly against the clock now. Her hands shook. She was shot to hell. Maxine was complaining of a blister on her little toe. Dorrie ran off upstairs like a heifer for the plaster roll and cut a strip and carefully fit it round the pea-sized top joint of the toe. Maxine moaned and screamed, tears squirted from her eyes, her face became a mask of grief as she felt the plaster arrangement inside her sock even more uncomfortable once strapped into her shoe. It all had to be removed again and a square quarter inch of plaster carefully applied like a miniature postage stamp to the reddened area.

'We're late,' hissed Dorrie, but even in the middle of this felt a great sick thud of relief that it was not two years ago when she had been racing against the clock to get to work pretending to them there that all this had not just happened. When at last she had caved in, when she had given in her notice, it felt like giving up the world, the flesh and the devil. It had been terrible at first, the loss of breadth, the loss of adult company. There were the minutes at various school gates with the other mothers, but you couldn't really call that proper talk, not with all the babies and toddlers on at them. After all she had not managed to keep both worlds up in the air. She knew she had failed.

She picked Robin up and jammed him into the buggy.

'Teeth!' said Martin, baring his own at her. 'You've forgotten about teeth!'

'Never mind,' she said through hers, gritted, manoeuvring the buggy across the front doorstep. 'Come on.'

'Why?' asked Martin, pulling his school jumper up to his

27

eyes and goggling at himself in front of the hall mirror.
'Burglars don't show their noses, Mum. Look. Mum.'

These days Martin flew off towards the playground as soon
as they reached the school gate, for which she was
profoundly grateful. For his first five years he had been full
of complaints, fault-finding and irritability. He still flew into
towering rages and hit her and screamed until he was pink
or blue in the face, often several times a day. As he was her
first child this had come as a shock. She even asked the
doctor about it, and the doctor had smiled and said his
sounded a fiery little nature but he would no doubt learn to
control himself in time. 'Also, all behaviour is *learned*
behaviour,' said the doctor reprovingly. 'Never shout back
or you'll just encourage him.' Plenty of the other mothers
had children who behaved similarly, she noticed after a
while. You just had to take it, and wait for time to pass. It
could take years. It did. He was loud, waspish, frequently
agitated and a constant prey to boredom. When she saw
him nibbling his nails, tired and white as a cross elf, she
would draw him onto her lap and make a basket of her
arms around him. She saw his lack of ease in the world,
and grieved for him, and knew it was her fault because she
was his mother.

Maxine was less irritable but more manipulative. Her
memory was terrifyingly precise and long – yesterday, for
example, she had raged at Dorrie for stealing a fruit
pastille, having remembered the colour of the top one from
several hours before. She relished experiments and emotional mayhem. Her new trick this week was to fix you with
her pale pretty eye, and say, quite coolly, 'I hate you.' This
poleaxed Dorrie. And yet this little girl was also utterly

unglazed against experience, as fresh and easily hurt as one of those new daffodil shoots.

Only when Robin was born had she realised what it was to have what is commonly known as an easy child. No rhyme nor reason to it. Same treatment, completely different. They were as they were as soon as they were born, utterly different from each other. That was something at least. It couldn't *all* be her fault.

Now it was halfway through Martin's first school year and he had settled in well. It was wonderful. She glanced in passing at other less fortunate mothers talking low and urgent with their infants, entwined and unlinking, like lovers, bargaining with furtive tears, sobs, clinging arms, angry rejections, pettishness and red eyes.

It was the same when she dropped Maxine off at nursery school half an hour later. On the way out she and Robin passed a little girl of three or so saying to her mother, 'But Mummy I *miss* you;' and the mother, smartly dressed, a briefcase by her, rather tightly reasoning with her, murmuring, glancing at her watch. Dorrie felt herself break into a light sympathetic sweat.

The little scene brought back Robin's trial morning there last week. He had refused to walk through the nursery school's entrance and was shouting and struggling as she carried him in. She had set him down by a low table of jigsaw puzzles and told him sternly that she would sit over there in that corner for five minutes, that his sister was just over there in the Wendy house, and that he must let her go quietly. From the toy kitchen he had brought her a plastic cupcake with a fat ingratiating smile.

'Here y'are,' he'd said.

'Save it for when I come to pick you up,' Dorrie had

said, handing it back to him, pity and coldness battling through her like warring blood corpuscles. At last he had given her a resigned kiss on the cheek and gone off to the painting table without another look. (Two hours alone, for the first time in months. Wait till he's at school, said the mothers; you won't know yourself.) She dashed a tear away, sneering at her own babyishness.

Now, today, there was this precious time with Robin. He liked to be around her, within a few yards of her, to keep her in his sight, but he did not pull the stuffing out of her as the other two did. He did not demand her thoughts and full attention like Maxine; nor that she should identify and change colour like litmus paper with his every modulation of emotion as it occurred, which was what Martin seemed to need. Sometimes those two were so extravagantly exacting, they levied such a fantastic rate of slavish fealty that they left her gasping for air.

No, Robin talked to his allies and foes, *sotto voce*, in the subterranean fields which ran alongside the privet-hedged landscape in which they moved together. He sent out smiles or little waves while Dorrie was working, and took breaks for a hug or to pause and drink squash, him on her lap like a stalwart beanbag.

She sorted the dirty whites from the coloured wash up on the landing, and he put them into the washing basket for her. Up and down the stairs she went with round baskets of washing, the smell of feet and bottoms, five sets, fresh and smelly, all different. Robin stuffed the garments into the washing machine one by one, shutting the door smartly and saying 'There!' and smiling with satisfaction. She did some handwashing at the sink, and he pushed a chair over across the floor to stand on, and squeezed the garments, then took handfuls of the soap bubbles that wouldn't drain away and trotted to and from the bucket on the mat with them.

'What a helpful boy you are!' she said. He beamed.

'Now I'm going to iron some things including Daddy's shirt for tonight,' she said. 'So you must sit over there because the iron is dangerous.'

'Hot,' he agreed, with a sharp camp intake of breath.

He sat down on the floor with some toys in a corner of the kitchen and as she ironed she looked over now and then at his soft thoughtfully frowning face as he tried to put a brick into a toy car, the curve of his big soft cheek like a mushroom somehow, and his lovely close-to-the-head small ears. He gave an unconscious sigh of concentration; his frequent sighs came right from deep in the diaphragm. Squab or chub or dab had been the words which best expressed him until recently, but now he was growing taller and fining down, his limbs had lost their chubbiness and his body had become his own.

No longer could she kiss his eyelids whenever she wished, nor pretend to bite his fingers, nor even stroke his hair with impunity. He was a child now, not a baby, and must be accorded his own dignity. The baby was gone, almost.

Abruptly she put the iron on its heel and swooped down on him, scooped him up and buried her nose in his neck with throaty growling noises. He huffed and shouted and laughed as they swayed struggling by the vegetable rack. She tickled him and they sank down to the lino laughing and shouting, then he rubbed his barely-there velvet nose against hers like an Eskimo, his eyes close and dark and

31

merry, inches from hers, gazing in without shame or constraint.

It was going to be a long series of leave-takings from now on, she thought; goodbye and goodbye and goodbye; that had been the case with the others, and now this boy was three and a half. Unless she had another. But then Max would leave. Or so he said. This treacherous brainless greed for more of the same, it would finish her off if she wasn't careful. If she wasn't already.

She took Max's shirt upstairs on a hanger and put the rest of the ironing away. What would she wear tonight? She looked at her side of the wardrobe. Everything that wasn't made of T-shirt or sweatshirt fabric was too tight for her now. Unenthusiastically she took down an old red shirt-dress, looser than the rest, and held it up against her reflection in the full-length mirror. She used to know what she looked like, she used to be interested. Now she barely recognised herself. She peeled off her sweatshirt and jeans and pulled the dress on. She looked enormous. The dress was straining at the seams. She looked away fast, round the bedroom, the unmade bed like a dog basket, the mess everywhere, the shelves of books on the wall loaded with forbidden fruit, impossible to broach, sealed off by the laws of necessity from her maternal eyes. During the past five years, reading a book had become for her an activity engaged in at somebody else's expense.

The doorbell rang and she answered it dressed as she was. Robin hid behind her.

'Gemma's got to be a crocodile tomorrow,' said Sally, who lived two roads away. 'We're desperate for green tights, I've tried Mothercare and Boots and then I thought of Maxine. I don't suppose?'

'Sorry,' said Dorrie, 'Only red or blue.'

'Worth a try,' said Sally, hopeless. 'You look dressed up.'

'I look fat,' said Dorrie. 'Wedding anniversary,' she added tersely.

'Ah,' said Sally. 'How many years?'

'Eight,' said Dorrie. 'Bronze. Sally, can you remember that feeling before all the family stuff kicked in, I know it's marvellous but. You know, that spark, that feeling of fun and – and lightness, somehow.'

Immediately Sally replied, 'It's still there in me but I don't know for how much longer.'

'You could try Verity,' said Dorrie. 'I seem to remember she put Hannah in green tights last winter to go with that holly berry outfit.'

'So she did!' said Sally. 'I'll give her a ring.'

'Kill,' whispered Robin, edging past the women into the tiny front garden; 'Die, megazord,' and he crushed a snail shell beneath his shoe. Half hidden beneath the windowsill he crouched in a hero's cave. Across the dangerous river of the front path he had to save his mother, who was chatting to a wicked witch. He started round the grape hyacinths as though they were on fire and squeezed his way along behind the lilac bush, past cobwebs and worms, until he burst out fiercely into the space behind the hedge. She was being forced to walk the plank. He leaped into the ocean and cantered sternly across the waves.

They were late coming out of nursery school, and Dorrie stood with the other mothers and nannies in the queue. Some were chatting, some were sagging and gazing into the middle distance.

33

In front of her, two women were discussing a third just out of earshot.

'Look at her nails,' said the one directly in front of Dorrie. 'You can always tell. Painted fingernails mean a rubbish mother.'

'I sometimes put nail polish on if I'm going out in the evening,' said the other.

'*If,*' scoffed the first. 'Once in a blue moon. And then you make a mess of it, I bet. You lose your touch. Anyway, you've got better things to do with your time, you give your time to your children, not to primping yourself up.'

Robin pushed his head between Dorrie's knees and clutched her thighs, a mini Atlas supporting the world.

Dorrie saw it was Patricia from Hawthornden Avenue.

'*I* was thinking of doing my nails today,' said Dorrie.

'What on earth *for?*' laughed Patricia. She was broad in the beam, clever but narrow-minded.

'Wedding anniversary,' said Dorrie. 'Out for a meal.'

'There you are then,' said Patricia triumphantly, as though she had proved some point.

'I had a blazing row with *my* husband last night,' said Patricia's friend. 'And I was just saying to myself, Right that's it, I was dusting myself down ready for the off, when I thought, No, hang on a minute, I *can't* go. I've got three little children, I've *got* to stay.'

Patricia's eyebrows were out of sight, she reeled from side to side laughing. They all laughed, looking sideways at each other, uneasy.

'Have you noticed what happens now that everyone's splitting up,' snorted Patricia's friend. 'I've got friends, their divorce comes through and do you know they say it's amazing! They lose weight and take up smoking and have all the weekends to themselves to do *whatever they want* in because the men take the children off out then.'

'Divorce,' said Dorrie ruminatively. 'Yes. You get to thirty-seven, married, three kids, and you look in the mirror, at least I did this morning, and you realise – it's a shock – you realise nothing else is supposed to happen until you die. Or you spoil the pattern.'

The nursery school doors opened at last. Dorrie held her arms out and Maxine ran into them. Maxine had woken screaming at five that morning, clutching her ear, but then the pain had stopped and she had gone back to sleep again. Dorrie had not. That was when she had gone downstairs and into the garden.

'The doctor's going to fit us in after her morning surgery, so I must run,' said Dorrie, scooping Maxine up to kiss her, strapping Robin into the buggy.

'Mum,' called Maxine, as they galloped slowly along the pavement, 'Mum, Gemma says I must only play with her or she won't be my friend. But I told her Suzanne was my best friend. Gemma's only second best.'

'Yes,' said Dorrie. 'Mind that old lady coming towards us.'

'Suzanne and me really wanted Gemma to play Sour Lemons but Shoshaya wanted her to play rabbits,' panted Maxine. 'Then Shoshaya cried and she told Miss Atkinson. And Miss Atkinson told us to let her play. But Gemma wanted to play Sour Lemons with me and Suzanne and she did.'

'Yes,' said Dorrie. She must get some milk, and extra cheese for lunch. She ought to pick up Max's jacket from the cleaners. Had she got the ticket? Had she got enough cash? Then there was Max's mother's birthday present to be bought and packed up and posted off to Salcombe, and a card. She had to be thinking of other people all the time or the whole thing fell apart. It was like being bitten all over by soldier ants without being able to work up enough interest to deal with them. Sometimes she found herself holding her breath for no reason at all.

'Why do you always say yes?' said Maxine.

'What?' said Dorrie. They stood at the kerb waiting to cross. She looked up at the top deck of the bus passing on the other side and saw a young man sitting alone up there. He happened to meet her eye for a moment as she stood with the children, and the way he looked at her, through her, as though she were a greengrocer's display or a parked car, made her feel less than useless. She was a rock or stone or tree. She was nothing.

'Why do you always say yes?' said Maxine.

'What?' said Dorrie.

'Why do you always say YES!' screamed Maxine in a rage.

'Cross *now*,' said Dorrie, grabbing her arm and hauling her howling across the road as she pushed the buggy.

They turned the corner into the road where the surgery was and saw a small boy running towards them trip and go flying, smack down onto the pavement.

'Oof,' said Maxine and Robin simultaneously.

The child held up his grazed hands in grief and started to split the air with his screams. His mother came lumbering up with an angry face.

'I told you, didn't I? I told you! You see? God was looking down and he saw you were getting out of control. You wouldn't do what I said, would you. And God said, *right*, and He made you fall down like that and that's what

36

happens when you're like that. So now maybe you'll listen the next time!'

Dorrie looked away, blinking. That was another thing, it had turned her completely soft. The boy's mother yanked him up by the arm, and dragged him past, moralising greedily over his sobs.

'She should have hugged him, Mummy, shouldn't she,' said Maxine astutely.

'Yes,' said Dorrie, stopping to blow her nose.

The tattered covers of the waiting room magazines smiled over at them in a congregation of female brightness and intimacy. The women I see in the course of a day, thought Dorrie, and it's women only (except Max at the end of the day), we can't really exchange more than a sentence or two of any interest because of our children. At this age they need us all the time; and anyway we often have little in common except femaleness and being in the same boat. Why should we? She scanned the leadlines while Robin and Maxine chose a book from the scruffy pile – 'How to dump him: twenty ways that work', 'Your hair: what does it say about you?' 'Countdown to your best orgasm.' Those were the magazines for the under-thirties, the free-standing feisty girls who had not yet crossed the ego line. And of course some girls never did cross the ego line. Like men, they stayed the stars of their own lives. Then there was this lot, this lot here with words like juggle and struggle across their covers, these were for her and her like – 'Modern motherhood: how do you measure up?'; 'Is your husband getting enough: time management and you'; 'Doormat etiquette: are you too nice?'

Am I too *nice*? thought Dorrie. They even took *that* away.

Nice here meant weak and feeble, *she* knew what it meant. Nice was now an insult, whereas self had been the dirty word when she was growing up. For girls, anyway. She had been trained to think of her mother and not be a nuisance. She couldn't remember ever saying (let alone being asked) what she wanted. To the point of thinking she didn't really mind what she wanted as long as other people were happy. It wasn't long ago.

The doctor inspected Maxine's eardrum with her pointed torch, and offered a choice.

'You can leave it and hope it goes away. That's what they'd do on the Continent.'

'But then it might flare up in the night and burst the eardrum. That happened to Martin. Blood on the pillow. Two sets of grommets since then.'

'Well, *tant pis*, they'd say. They're tough on the Continent. Or it's the usual Amoxcyllin.'

'I don't like to keep giving them that. But perhaps I could have some in case it gets very painful later. And not give it otherwise.'

'That's what I'd do,' said the doctor, scribbling out a prescription.

'How are you finding it, being back at work?' asked Dorrie timidly but with great interest. The doctor had just returned after her second baby and second five-month maternity leave.

'Fine, fine,' smiled the doctor, rubbing her eyes briefly, tired blue eyes kind in her worn face. 'In fact of course it's easier. I mean, it's hard in terms of organisation, hours, being at full stretch. But it's still easier than being at home. With tiny children you really have to be so . . . selfless.'

'Yes,' said Dorrie, encouraged. 'It gets to be a habit. In

the end you really do lose yourself. Lost. But then they start
to be not tiny.'

'Lost!' said Maxine. 'Who's lost? What you talking
about, Mum? *Who's* lost?'

The doctor glanced involuntarily at her watch.

'I'm sorry,' said Dorrie, bustling the children over to the
door.

'Not at all,' said the doctor. She did look tired. 'Look
after yourself.'

Look after yourself, thought Dorrie as she walked the
children home, holding her daughter's hand as she skipped
and pulled at her. She glanced down at her hand holding
Maxine's, plastic shopping bags of vegetables over her
wrist, and her nails looked uneven, not very clean.
According to the nursery school queue, that meant she was
a good mother. She did nothing for herself. She was a
vanity-free zone. Broken nails against that tight red dress
wouldn't be very alluring, but all that was quite beyond her
now. By schooling herself to harmlessness, constant usefulness to others, she had become a big fat zero.

By the time they got home Dorrie was carrying Robin
straddled African-style across her front, and he was
alternately sagging down protesting, then straightening his
back and climbing her like a tree. He had rebelled against
the buggy, so she had folded it and trailed it behind her,
but when he walked one of his shoes hurt him; she knew
the big toenail needed cutting but whenever his feet were
approached he set up a herd-of-elephants roar. She made a
mental note to creep up with the scissors while he slept. I
can't see how the family would work if I let myself start
wanting things again, thought Dorrie; give me an inch and
I'd run a mile, that's what I'm afraid of.

*

39

Indoors, she peeled vegetables while they squabbled and played around her legs. She wiped the surfaces while answering long strings of zany questions which led up a spiral staircase into the wild blue nowhere.

'I know when you're having a thought, Mummy,' said Maxine astutely. 'Because when I start to say something then you close your eyes.'

'Can I have my Superman suit?' said Robin.

'In a minute,' said Dorrie, who was tying up a plastic sack of rubbish.

'Not in a minute,' said Robin. '*Now.*'

The thing about small children was that they needed things all day long. They wanted games set up and tears wiped away and a thousand small attentions. This was all fine until you started to do something else round them, or something that wasn't just a basic menial chore, she thought, dragging the hoover out after burrowing in the stacking boxes for the Superman suit. You had to be infinitely elastic and adaptable; all very laudable but this had the concomitant effect of slowly but surely strangling your powers of concentration.

Then Superman needed help in blowing his nose, and next he wanted his cowboys and Indians reached down from the top of the cupboard. She forgot what she was thinking about.

Now she was chopping onions finely as thread so that Martin would not be able to distinguish their texture in the meatballs and so spit them out. (Onions were good for their immune systems, for their blood.) She added these to the minced lamb and mixed in eggs and breadcrumbs then shaped the mixture into forty tiny globes, these to bubble away in a tomato sauce, one of her half-dozen flesh-concealing ruses against Maxine's incipient vegetarianism. (She knew it was technically possible to provide enough protein for young children from beans as long as these were eaten in various careful conjunctions with other beans – all to do with amino acids – but she was not wanting to plan and prepare even more separate meals – Max had his dinner later in the evening – not just yet anyway – or she'd be simmering and peeling till midnight.)

The whole pattern of family life hung for a vivid moment above the chopping board as a seamless cycle of nourishment and devoural. And after all, children were not teeth extracted from you. Perhaps it was necessary to be devoured.

Dorrie felt sick and faint as she often did at this point in the day, so she ate a pile of tepid left-over mashed potato and some biscuits while she finished clearing up and peace-keeping. The minutes crawled by. She wanted to lie down on the lino and pass out.

Maxine's nursery school crony, Suzanne, came to play after lunch. Dorrie helped them make a shop and set up tins of food and jars of dried fruit, but they lost interest after five minutes and wanted to do colouring in with felt tips. Then they had a fight over the yellow. Then they played with the Polly Pockets, and screamed, and hit each other. Now, now, said Dorrie, patient but intensely bored, as she pulled them apart and calmed them down and cheered them up.

At last it was time to drop Suzanne off and collect Martin. Inside the school gates they joined the other mothers, many of whom Dorrie now knew by name or by their child's name, and waited at the edge of the playground for the release of their offspring.

41

'I can't tell you anything about Wednesday until Monday,' said Thomas' mother to a woman named Marion. A note had been sent back in each child's reading folder the previous day, announcing that the last day before half term would finish at twelve. The women who had part-time jobs now started grumbling about this, and making convoluted webs of arrangements. 'If you drop Neil off at two then my neighbour will be there, you remember, he got on with her last time all right, that business with the spacehopper; then Verity can drop Kirsty by after Tumble-tots and I'll be back with Michael and Susan just after three-thirty. Hell! It's ballet. Half an hour later. Are you *sure* that's all right with you?'

'They're late,' said Thomas' mother, glancing at her watch.

'So your youngest will be starting nursery after Easter,' said Marion to Dorrie. 'You won't know yourself.'

'No,' said Dorrie. She reached down to ruffle Robin's feathery hair; he was playing around her legs.

'Will you get a job then?' asked Marion.

'Um, I thought just for those weeks before summer I'd get the house straight, it's only two hours in the morning. And a half,' said Dorrie in a defensive rush. 'Collect my thoughts. If there are any.'

'Anyway, you do your husband's paperwork in the evenings, don't you?' said Thomas' mother. 'The accounts and that. VAT.'

'You get so you can't see the wood for the trees, don't you,' said Dorrie. 'You get so good at fitting things round everything else. Everybody else.'

'I used to be in accounts,' said Marion. 'B.C. But I couldn't go back now. I've lost touch. I couldn't get into my suits any more, I tried the other day. I couldn't do it! I'd hardly cover the cost of the childcare. I've lost my nerve.'

'My husband says he'll back me up one hundred per cent when the youngest starts school,' said Thomas' mother pensively. 'Whatever job I want to do. But no way would he be able to support change which would end by making his working life more difficult, he said.'

'That's not really on, then, is it?' said Marion. 'Unless you get some nursery school work to fit round school hours. Or turn into a freelance something.'

'Some people seem to manage it,' said Thomas' mother. 'Susan Gloverall.'

'I didn't know she was back at work.'

'Sort of. She's hot-desking somewhere off the A3, leaves the kids with a childminder over Tooting way. Shocking journey, but the devil drives.'

'Keith still not found anything, then? That's almost a year now.'

'I know. Dreadful really. I don't think it makes things any, you know, easier between them. And of course she can't leave the kids with him while he's looking. Though she said he's watching a lot of TV.'

'What about Nicola Beaumont, then?' said Dorrie.

'Oh her,' said Marion. 'Wall-to-wall nannies. No thank you.'

'I could never make enough to pay a nanny,' said Thomas' mother. 'I never earned that much to start with. And then you have to pay their tax on top, out of your own taxed income. You'd have to earn eighteen thousand at least before you broke even if you weren't on the fiddle. I've worked it out.'

'Nearer twenty-two these days,' said Marion, 'In London. Surely.'

'Nicola's nice though,' said Dorrie. 'Her daughter Jade, the teenage one, she's babysitting for us tonight.'

'Well she never seems to have much time for me,' said Marion.

'I think she just doesn't have much time full stop,' said Dorrie.

'Nor do any of us, dear,' said Thomas' mother. 'Not *proper* time.'

'Not time to yourself,' said Marion.

'I bet she gets more of that than I do. She commutes, doesn't she? There you are then!'

They were all laughing again when the bell went.

'Harry swallowed his tooth today,' said Martin. 'Mrs Tyrone said it didn't matter, it would melt inside him.' He wiggled his own front tooth, an enamel tag, tipping it forward with his fingernail. Soon there would be the growing looseness, the gradual twisting of it into a spiral, hanging on by a thread, and the final silent snap.

'He won't get any money from the Tooth Fairy, will he, Mum,' said Martin. 'Will he, Mum? Will he, Mum? Mum. Mum!'

'Yes,' said Dorrie. 'What? I expect so dear.' She was peeling carrots and cutting them into sticks.

'And Kosenia scratched her bandage off today, and she's got eczema, and she scratched off, you know, that stuff on top, like the cheese on Shepherd's Pie, she just lifted it off,' Martin went on.

'Crust,' said Dorrie.

'Yes, crust,' said Martin. 'I'm not eating those carrots. No way.'

'Carrots are very good for you,' said Dorrie. 'And tomorrow I'm going to pack some carrot sticks in your lunch box and I want you to eat them.'

'Hey yeah right,' gabbled Martin. 'Hey yeah right get a life!'

And he marched off to where the other two were watching a story about a mouse who ate magic berries and grew as big as a lion. Television was nothing but good and hopeful and stimulating compared with the rest of life so far as she could see. Certainly it had been the high point of her own childhood. Her mother thought she spoiled her children, but then most of her friends said their mothers thought the same about them. She was trying to be more tender with them – she and her contemporaries – to offer them choices rather than just tell them what to do; to be more patient and to hug them when they cried, rather than briskly talk of being brave; never to hit them. They felt, they all felt they were trying harder than their parents had ever done, to love well. And one of the side effects of this was that their children were incredibly quick to castigate any shortfall in the quality of attention paid to them.

Now they were fighting again. Martin was screaming and chattering of injustice like an angry ape. Maxine shrilled back at him with her ear-splitting screech. Robin sat on the ground, hands to his ears, sobbing deep-chested sobs of dismay.

She groaned with boredom and frustration. Really she could not afford to let them out of her sight yet; not for another six months, anyway; not in another room, even with television.

'Let's all look at pictures of Mummy and Daddy getting married,' she shouted above the din, skilfully deflecting the furies. Sniffing and shuddering they eventually allowed themselves to be gathered round the album she had dug out, while she wiped their eyes and noses and clucked mild reproaches. The thing was, it did not do simply to turn off. She was not a part of the action but her involved presence was required as it was necessary for her to be ready at any point to step in as adjudicator. What did not work was when she carried on round them, uninvolved, doing the chores, thinking her own thoughts and making placatory noises when the din grew earsplitting. Then the jaws of anarchy opened wide.

Soon they were laughing at the unfamiliar images of their parents in the trappings of romance, the bright spirited faces and trim figures.

'Was it the best day in your life?' asked Maxine.

There was me, she thought, looking at the photographs; there used to be me. She was the one who'd put on two stone; he still looked pretty fit. The whole process would have been easier, she might have been able to retain some self-respect, if at some point there had been a formal handing over like Hong Kong.

At the end of some days, by the time each child was breathing regularly, asleep, she would stand and wait for herself to grow still, and the image was of an ancient vase, crackle-glazed, still in one piece but finely crazed all over its surface. I'm shattered, she would groan to Max on his return, hale and whole, from the outside world.

Now, at the end of just such a day, Dorrie was putting the children down while Max had a bath after his day at work.

It was getting late. She had booked a table at L'Horizon and arranged for Jade to come round and babysit at eight. They had not been out together for several months, but Dorrie had not forgotten how awful it always was.

It was twenty to eight, and Robin clung to her.

'Don't go, Mummy, don't go,' he sobbed, jets of water spouting from his eyes, his mouth a square buckle of anguish.

'Don't be silly,' said Dorrie, with her arms round him. 'I've got to go and change, darling. I'll come straight back.'

'No you won't,' he bellowed. Martin watched with interest, nibbling his nails.

'He's making me feel sad, Mum,' commented Maxine. 'I feel like crying now too.'

'So do I,' said Dorrie grimly.

'What's all the noise?' demanded Max, striding into the room drubbing his hair with a towel. 'Why aren't you children asleep yet?'

Robin took a wild look at his father and, howling with fresh strength, tightened his grip on Dorrie with arms, legs and fingers.

'Let go of your mother this minute,' snarled Max in a rage, starting to prise away the desperate fingers one by one. Robin's sobs became screams, and Maxine started to cry.

'Please, Max,' said Dorrie. 'Please don't.'

'This is ridiculous,' hissed Max, wrenching him from her body. Dorrie watched the child move across the line into hysteria, and groaned.

'Stop it, Daddy!' screamed Martin, joining in, and downstairs the doorbell rang.

'Go and answer it then!' said Max, pinning his frantic three-year-old son to the bed.

'Oh God,' said Dorrie as she stumbled downstairs to open the door to the babysitter.

'Hello, Jade!' she said with a wild fake smile. 'Come in!'

'Sounds like I'm a bit early,' said Jade, stepping into the hall, tall and slender and dressed in snowy-white shirt and jeans.

'No, no, let me show you how to work the video, that's just the noise they make on their way to sleep,' said Dorrie, feeling herself bustle around like a fat dwarf. It seemed pathetic that she should be going out and this lovely girl staying in. The same thought had crossed Jade's mind, but she had her whole life ahead of her, as everyone kept saying.

'Any problems, anything at all, if one of them wakes and asks for me, please ring and I'll come back, it's only a few minutes away.'

'Everything'll be *fine*,' said Jade, as if to a fussy infant. 'You shouldn't worry so much.'

'I'll swing for that child,' they heard Max growl from the landing, then a thundering patter of feet, and febrile shrieks.

'Eight years, eh,' said Max across the candlelit damask. 'My Old Dutch. No need to look so tragic.'

Dorrie was still trying to quiet her body's alarm system, the waves of miserable heat, the klaxons of distress blaring in her bloodstream from Robin's screams.

'You've got to go out sometimes,' said Max. 'It's getting ridiculous.'

'I'm sorry I didn't manage to make myself look nice,'

said Dorrie. '*You* look nice. Anyway, it's four pounds an hour. It's like sitting in a taxi.'

Max was big and warm, sitting relaxed like a sportsman after the game, but his eyes were flinty.

'It's just arrogant, thinking that nobody else can look after them as well as you,' he said.

'They can't,' mumbled Dorrie, under her breath.

'You're a dreadful worrier,' said Max. 'You're always worrying.'

'Well,' said Dorrie. 'Somebody's got to.'

'Everything would carry on all right, you know, if you stopped worrying.'

'No it wouldn't. I wish it would. But it wouldn't.'

Lean and sexually luminous young waiting staff glided gracefully around them.

'Have you chosen,' he said, and while she studied the menu he appraised her worn face, free of make-up except for an unaccustomed and unflattering application of lipstick, and the flat frizz of her untended hair. She was starting to get a double chin, he reflected wrathfully; she had allowed herself to put on more weight. Here he was on his wedding anniversary sitting opposite a fat woman. And if he ever said anything, *she* said, the children. It showed a total lack of respect; for herself; for him.

'I just never seem to get any time to myself,' muttered Dorrie, nudged by the shade of her former self which had that morning appeared to rise up like a living ghost in the garden crossing the lawn to meet her, and to whom she had as good as promised a reunion. She felt uneasy complaining. Once she'd stopped bringing in money she knew she'd lost the right to object. So did he.

'It's a matter of discipline,' said Max, sternly.

49

He felt a terrible restlessness at this time of year, particularly since his fortieth. The birthday cards had all been about being past it. Mine's a pint of Horlicks, jokes about bad backs, expanding waistlines, better in candle-light. There it stretched, all mapped out for him; a long or not-so-long march to the grave; and he was forbidden from looking to left or right. He had to hold himself woodenly impervious, it would seem, since every waking moment was supposed to be a married one. All right for her, she could stun herself with children. But he needed a romantic motive or life wasn't worth living.

He could see the food and drink and television waiting for him at each day's end, and the thickening of middle age, but he was buggered if he was going to let himself go down that route. He watched Dorrie unwisely helping herself to sautéed potatoes. Her body had become like a car to her, he thought, it got her around, it accommodated people at various intervals, but she herself seemed to have nothing to do with it any more. She just couldn't be bothered.

What had originally drawn him to her was the balance between them, a certain tranquil buoyancy she had which had gone well with his own more explosive style. These days she was not so much tranquil as stagnant, while all the buoyancy had been bounced off. He wished he could put a bomb under her. She seemed so apathetic except when she was loving the children. It made him want to boot her broad bottom whenever she meandered past him in the house, just to speed her up.

The children had taken it out of her, he had to admit. She'd had pneumonia after Maxine, her hair had fallen out in handfuls after Robin, there had been two Caesarians, plus that operation to remove an ovarian cyst. The saga of her health since babies was like a seaside postcard joke, along with the mothers-in-law and the fat-wife harridans. After that childminder incident involving Martin breaking his leg at the age of two, she'd done bits of part-time but even that had fizzled out soon after Robin, so now she wasn't bringing in any money at all. When he married her, she'd had an interesting job, she'd earned a bit, she was lively and sparky; back in the mists of time. Now he had the whole pack of them on his back and he was supposed to be as philosophical about this as some old leech-gatherer.

He didn't want to hurt her, that was the trouble. He did not want the house to fly apart in weeping and wailing and children who would plead with him not to go, Daddy. He did not want to seem disloyal, either. But, he thought wildly, neither could he bear being sentenced to living death. Things were going to have to be different. She couldn't carry on malingering round the house like this. It wasn't fair. She shouldn't expect. He felt a shocking contraction of pity twist his guts. Why couldn't she bloody well look after herself better? He took a deep breath.

'Did I mention about Naomi,' he said casually, spearing a floret of broccoli.

Naomi was Max's right-hand woman at the builder's yard. She oversaw the stock, manned the till when necessary, sorted the receipts and paperwork for Dorrie to deal with at home and doled out advice about undercoats to the customers. She had been working for them for almost two years.

'Is she well?' asked Dorrie. 'I thought she was looking very white when I saw her last Wednesday.'

'Not only is she not well, she's throwing up all over the

place,' said Max heavily. 'She's pregnant,' he added in a muffled voice, stuffing more vegetables into his mouth.

'Pregnant?' said Dorrie. 'Oh!' Tears came to her eyes and she turned to scrabble under the table as if for a dropped napkin. So far she had managed to hide from him her insane lusting after yet another.

'That's what I thought,' sighed Max, misinterpreting her reaction.

'I'm so pleased for her, they've been wanting a baby for ages,' said Dorrie, and this time it was her voice that was muffled.

'So of course I've had to let her go,' said Max, looking at his watch.

'You've *what?*' said Dorrie.

'It's a great shame, of course. I'll have to go through all that with someone else now, showing them the ropes and so on.'

'How *could* you, Max?'

'Look, I knew you'd be like this. I *know*. It's a shame isn't it, yes; but there it is. That's life. It's lucky it happened when it did. Another few weeks and she'd have been able to nail me to the wall, unfair dismissal, the works.'

'But they need the money,' said Dorrie, horrified. 'How are they going to manage the mortgage now?'

'He should pull his finger out then, shouldn't he.' shrugged Max. 'He's public sector anyway, they'll be all right. Look, Dorrie, I've got a wife and children to support.'

'Get her back,' said Dorrie. 'Naomi will be fine. She's not like me, she'll have the baby easily, she won't get ill afterwards, nor will the baby. We were unlucky. She's very capable, she's not soft about things like childminders. You'd be mad to lose her.'

'Actually,' said Max, 'I've offered her a part-time job when she is ready to come back, and I rather think that might suit us better too. If I keep her below a certain number of hours.'

'What did Naomi say to *that*?'

'She was still a bit peeved about being let go,' said Max. 'But she said she'd think about it. If she could combine it with another part-time job. Beggars can't be choosers. I mean, if she chooses to have a baby, that's her choice.'

'I see,' said Dorrie carefully. 'So who will take over her work at the yard meanwhile?'

'Well, you, of course,' said Max, swallowing a big forkful of chop, his eyes bulging. He hurried on. 'Robin starts at nursery after Easter, Maxine's nearly finished there, and Martin's doing fine at school full-time now. So you can work the mornings, then you can collect Robin and Maxine and bring them along for a sandwich and work round them from then till it's time to pick up Martin. We can leave the paperwork till the evening. We'll save all ways like that. He's a big boy now, he can potter around.'

'He's only three and a half,' she said breathlessly. 'And when would I do the meals and the ironing and the cleaning and the shopping in all this?'

'Fit it in round the edges,' said Max. 'Other women do. It'll be good for you, get you out of the house. Come on, Dorrie, I can't carry passengers forever. You'll have to start pulling your weight again.'

It was towards the end of the main course and they had both drunk enough house white to be up near the surface.

'They're hard work, young children, you know,' she said.

'You said yourself they're getting easier every day. You said so yourself. It's not like when they were all at home all day screaming their heads off.'

'It is when they're on holiday,' she said. 'That's nearly twenty weeks a year, you know. What happens *then*?'

'You're off at a tangent again,' he said, sighing, then demanded, 'What *do* you want out of life?'

'It's not some sort of anaconda you've got to wrestle with,' said Dorrie. She realised that this latest sequestration of her hours would send her beside herself. Loss of inner life, that's what it was; lack of any purchase in the outside world, and loss of all respect; continuous unavoidable Lilliputian demands; numbness, apathy and biscuits. She was at the end of her rope.

'We can't just wait for things to fall into our laps though,' said Max, thinking about his own life.

'We're doing all right,' said Dorrie.

'That doesn't mean to say we couldn't do better. We need to expand.'

'We're managing the mortgage,' said Dorrie. 'I think we should be grateful.'

'That's the spirit,' said Max. 'That's the spirit that made this island great. Stand and stare, eh. Stand and stare.'

'What would you prefer?' said Dorrie. 'Life's a route march, then you die?'

'But then *you've* got what you wanted, haven't you – the children.'

'You are horrible,' said Dorrie. She took a great gulp of wine and drained her glass. 'It's about how well you've loved and how well you've been loved.' She didn't sound very convincing, she realised, in fact she sounded like Thought for the Day. She sounded like some big sheep bleating.

'I don't know what it is, Dorrie,' he said sadly, 'But you're all damped down. You've lost your spirit. You're not there any more.'

'I know. I know. But that's what I'm trying to say. You think I've just turned into a boring saint. But I'm still there. If you could just take them for a few hours now and then and be *nice* to them, if I just had a bit of quiet time . . .'

'I'm not exactly flourishing either, you know. You're getting to me.'

'Sorry. Sorry. I seem to be so dreary these days. But . . .'

'That's what I mean. Such a victim. Makes me want to kick you.'

'Don't Max. Please don't. We've got to go back to that girl and pay her first.'

'Just being miserable and long-suffering, you think that'll make me sorry for you.'

'Max . . .'

'But it makes me hate you, if you must know.'

Back at the house, Max handed Dorrie his wallet and went off upstairs. He was tired as he brushed his teeth, and angry at the way the evening had gone; nor did he like his bad-tempered reflection in the bathroom mirror. Soon he was asleep, frowning in release like a captive hero.

Dorrie meanwhile was fumbling with five-pound notes, enquiring brightly as to whether Jade had had a quiet evening.

'Oh yes, there wasn't a sound out of them once you'd gone,' said Jade, not strictly truthfully, still mesmerised by the beautiful eyes of the sex murderer with the razor on the screen. There had actually been a noise from the boys' bedroom and when she had put her head around the door sure enough the younger one was lying in a pool of sick. But he was breathing fine so she left him to it, it wasn't bothering him and no way was she going to volunteer for that sort of thing. She was getting paid to babysit, not to do stuff like that. That would have been right out of order.

'Would you like to stay and finish your video?' asked Dorrie politely, flinching as she watched the razor slit through filmstar flesh.

'No, that's all right,' said Jade reluctantly. She flicked the remote control and the bloody image disappeared. She sighed.

'Well, thank you again,' said Dorrie. 'It's lovely to know I can leave them with someone I can trust.'

'That's OK' said Jade. 'No problem.' And with a royal yawn she made her exit.

It took Dorrie half an hour or so to bathe the dazed Robin, to wash the acrid curds holding kernels of sweetcorn and discs of peas from his feathery hair and wrap him in clean pyjamas and lay him down in the big bed beside his noble-looking father, where he fell instantly asleep, slumbering on a cloud of beauty.

She kissed his warm face and turned back, her body creaking in protest, to the job in hand. Downstairs in the midnight kitchen she scraped the duvet cover and pillow case with the knife kept specifically for this purpose, dumping the half-digested chyme into the sink, running water to clear it away, then scraping again, gazing out of the window into the blackness of the wild garden, yearning at the spatter of rain on the glass and the big free trees out there with their branches in the sky.

Their needs were what was set. Surely that was the logic of it. It was for *her* to adapt, accommodate, modify in order to allow the familial organism to flourish. Here she was weeping over her own egotism like a novice nun, for goodness sake, except it was the family instead of God. But still it was necessary, selflessness, for a while, even if it made you spat on by the world. By your husband. By your children. By yourself.

She wanted to smash the kitchen window. She wanted to hurt herself. Her ghost was out there in the garden, the ghost from her freestanding past. If she kept up this business of reunion, it would catch hold of her hands and saw her wrists to and fro across the jagged glass. It would tear her from the bosom of this family she had breastfed. No. She must stay this side of the glass from now on, thickening and cooling like some old planet until at last she killed the demands of that self-regarding girl out there.

She twisted and squeezed water from the bedlinen she had just rinsed. If she were to let herself be angry about this obliteration, of her particular mind, of her own relish for things, then it would devour the family. Instead she must let it gnaw at her entrails like some resident tiger. This was not sanctimony speaking but necessity. All this she knew but could not explain. She was wringing the sheet with such force that it creaked.

'Fresh air,' she said aloud, and tried to open the window in front of her. It was locked, clamped tight with one of the antiburglar fastenings which they had fitted on all the windows last summer. She felt around in the cupboard above the refrigerator for the key, but it wasn't in its usual place. She hunted through the rows of mugs, the tins of tuna and tomatoes, the bags of rice and flour and pasta, and found it at last inside the glass measuring jug.

Leaning across the sink she unlocked the window and opened it onto the night. A spray of rain fell across her face and she gasped. There was the cold fresh smell of wet earth. It occurred to her that this might not necessarily be killer pain she was feeling, not terrible goodbyeforever pain as she had assumed; and she felt light-headed with the shock of relief.

Perhaps this was not the pain of wrist-cutting after all. Instead, the thought came to her, it might be the start of that intense outlandish sensation that comes after protracted sleep; the feeling in a limb that has gone numb, when blood starts to flow again, sluggishly at first, reviving; until after a long dormant while that limb is teeming again, tingling into life.

Out in the garden, out in the cold black air, she could see the big trees waving their wild bud-bearing branches at her.

Millennium Blues

There had been an unbelievable amount of talk about the weather, not to mention the end of the world and so on. The earth continued to turn round the sun, but only just, it seemed. Never before in all its history had the planet's atmosphere been so heavily matted with information about everything, so clotted with flashes and scoops and entreaties and jeremiads. The air and all its waves were sodden with chitchat.

Muscae volitantes, or flitting flies; that is the name for the spots which float before the eyes and stop you from reading. Muscae volitantes are what aeroplanes look like when viewed from high above. They are worse when you look up at them. On this 228th day of the year 1999, aircraft like stingray are floating overhead, roaring and screaming, their yellow eyes glaring down at the sleeping landscape beneath.

Seen from the air this ominous August dawn, the Thames is a diamond-dusted silver ribbon. The aircraft follow the river faithfully, nose to tail, as they descend over south-west London, giving panoramic views of the individual boat houses, Putney Bridge, the green spaces of the Hurlingham Club and Fulham Palace gardens, straining and whining as they throttle back over the salubrious complacence of Barnes, then whistling on through the malty cumulus clouds issuing from the chimneys of Mortlake's brewery. On they roar, hooting and wrangling across the four hundred botanic acres at Kew, from there to shade Richmond's millennial prosperity with their wings; then on down lower still to the shattered concentration of Hounslow, its double-glazed schools and uproarious bedrooms, where those on the ground can if they so desire look up and check the colour of the pilot's tie.

Until at last they touch down at Heathrow. All aircraft coming in to land here must first fly directly across the capital when the prevailing wind is blowing. It is an unusual arrangement which has not been much imitated by other countries, but without being unpleasantly nationalistic about this, the British have always been made of sterner stuff.

The planes still wear their lights like earrings in this no man's land between night and day. Cassie Withers stands in her Kew back garden and watches them cross the sky one after another, counting them instead of sheep. She was woken by the first flight in from Seoul. Today at some point her husband Steven Withers will be returning from his fifth foreign trip of the month. The constant overarching trajectories of noise accelerate and fade into one another. Two days ago Steven heard about a problem with the new bidets at one of his company's hotels in the Philippines. He tried phoning the local quality manager but got a voicemail because of the time difference.

'Can't it wait ten hours?' asked Cassie.

'I can *be* there in ten hours,' said Steven. 'That's the beauty of living here.'

And he had jumped on the next plane out.

Now Cassie gazes up beyond the planes as the sky grows lighter. Several stars are almost discernible through the dense maroon-tinted vapour of early morning. She'd watched a documentary on stars last night, about how the earth is long overdue collision with an asteroid or comet, just like the one that wiped out the dinosaurs. She had also learned from this programme that a Grand Cross of the planets is due this month, in the four fixed signs of the zodiac – Taurus, Aquarius, Scorpio, Leo – and that flat earthers everywhere are interpreting these signs as the four horsemen of the Apocalypse. Then she had gone to bed and read about Nostradamus – in the last months of this century it is quite hard *not* to read about Nostradamus, sixteenth-century Provençal plague doctor, and his 942-verse history of the world's future. She had lingered for a while over a particularly interesting couplet:

> The year 1999, the seventh month,
> From the sky will come a great King of Terror.

Nuclear war was joint favourite with an asteroid attack, according to the editor's note. Nostradamus had been right about several things so far, including the death of Henri II in a jousting accident and also the fall of Communism; so there was a strong possibility of *something* awful happening soon, it seemed.

It has been an unnaturally still hot summer, and even this early on Saturday there is no freshness in the garden. Cassie yawns and creaks and wonders whether she has M.E. or perhaps a brain tumour or some slow-growing cancer. But so many of her friends are dragging round in a similar state that she decides it must be the unrenewing air of these dogdays. Verity Freeling dropped dead last Tuesday without warning, extinguished by the three-week chest virus which has rampaged through everyone round here. It's said to come from China, and it simply laughs at antibiotics. Verity's husband is frantically trying to find a nanny for the three children before he loses his job.

Or perhaps it's just sleep. Because of the aircraft she has worn earplugs at night ever since moving to Kew ten years ago. Recently she went deaf as a result of the build-up of impacted wax. For a while she was quite pleased as this removed her from the constant din of aircraft and family life, and there were no side effects save the occasional muffled crump inside her head like a footstep in deep snow. Then reason had prevailed and her GP had syringed her ears. Unfortunately this had had a side effect – tinnitus – which is slowly driving her up the wall.

Sometimes this new ringing in her ears changes pitch, as now, and turns into a high silvery singing noise with a squeak to it like the edge hysteria gives a voice, or like the sharpening of angels' knives, stainless, at high speed.

'Mum, what comes after nineteen-ninety-nine?' asks her five-year-old son Peter as she clears up after breakfast. 'Is it nineteen-ninety-ten?'

'No,' says Cassie. 'Would you sort those knives and forks for me like a good boy. No. It goes nineteen-ninety-nine. TWO THOUSAND.'

'Mum,' he says, picking up a fork, frowning. 'Mum, will it be the end of the world then?'

'No of course not,' says Cassie heartily. 'It's just a

number. It doesn't actually mean anything at all. Unless you believe in Jesus.'

'Do you believe in Jesus?' he asks, as he sometimes does.

'I'm not sure,' she says diplomatically. 'Some people do. Auntie Katie does.'

'I believe in him,' he says staunchly.

'Well that's nice,' she says, then can't help asking, 'Why do you believe in him?'

'Because otherwise who *made* it,' he demands crossly. 'Of course.'

He marches out of the kitchen in a huff.

She finishes the dishes, then takes a cup of coffee into the front room where Peter is now lining up a row of small plastic dinosaurs behind the sofa while Michael, his elder brother, hunches over holiday homework in front of the television.

'It's only the news,' he says, forestalling her protest. 'It helps me concentrate.'

She sits by him and lets the news wash over her. Plague is spreading up from Greece through the Balkans, and now Venice has succumbed. There is footage of floods in China, drought in India, war in Africa, famine in Korea, fire in Australia, hysteria in America and desperation in Russia. Reports of a mass throat-cutting in the deserts of New Mexico are just starting to trickle in. Record temperatures worldwide, yet again, have led to speculation that the human race will become a nocturnal species in the next century, on the basis that it's cooler at night.

Later that morning Cassie leaves her boys playing Death-wish in the waiting room, and sees her doctor.

'Could it be tinnitus?' she asks as he peers inside.

'Tinnitus is just a word for any noise you can hear that other people can't.'

'So it *is* tinnitus.'

'Idiopathic tinnitus, if you want a loftier label.'

'Idiopathic?'

'It simply means there's no known cause,' he says, finishing his examination. 'No known cure either, I'm afraid. Just try to ignore it and hope it'll go away.'

'But that's awful!'

'At least you're not deaf as well. Deafness combined with tinnitus is very common in old age.'

'Does everybody have some sort of noise?' asks Cassie. 'Because I found myself thinking perhaps it was always there and I just didn't notice.'

'That is often exactly the case,' smiles the doctor approvingly. 'Something occurs in the ear, some small malfunction, and there it is: the noise revealed. Unmasked. There is a visual analogy. You come home one day and notice a neighbour's hideous new purple windowframes. You point them out to your husband. He looks at you in amazement and says, they've been like that for three years. Once you become aware of something, you can't easily lose that awareness.'

'Loss of innocence,' says Cassie.

'In a manner of speaking,' he replies. 'Yes.'

Cassie knows nine of her ten minutes are up, and decides not to use the last one trying to describe her recent feelings of intense foreboding. After all, he might feel he has to put her on Prozac.

They take sandwiches to the park for lunch. Cassie wrestles with each shouting boy in turn, applying sunblock, and then warns them not to roll down the grassy slope because of pesticides. She closes her eyes and feels the sun warm her shoulders, kiss her bare arms, and knows it is hostile, fake gold, full of malignant power.

Being out in the sun and the open air used to be health-giving. Now the sea is full of viruses, one bathe can leave you in a wheelchair for good; no wonder the fish have turned belly up this summer, bloated, to float and rot. As for sex, she thinks, watching her boys play, by the time it's their turn it'll be so dangerous they'll have to do it in wetsuits.

'You look a bit down,' says her friend Judith as she joins her on the park bench.

'Is it so obvious?' smiles Cassie. 'Talk about gloom and doom. I've got this horrible feeling that something appalling is about to happen.'

'When you think about it, something appalling always *is* happening, somewhere in the world,' says Judith, watching her daughters run over towards the swings. 'That's why I don't read the papers. I used to feel I ought to; that I *ought* to know about these terrible things. Then one day I just stopped. And my knowing or not knowing has made no difference at all to the state of the world.'

'How do you know?' says Cassie. 'We're all implicated.'

Judith merely smiles a smug smile. Pregnant with her third, she has been given 29 December as the date for the baby's arrival, but she is determined it will wait until the new century. She is going to call it Milly if it's a girl or Len if it's a boy.

'Did you hear about Sally Pimlott?' asks Judith, remembering some gossip. 'She handed out Lion bars at Ben's birthday party last week, she didn't realise they had nuts in, and one of the children had a fatal nut allergy and had to be rushed to hospital.'

'No!' breathed Cassie. 'And is it all right now?'

'Intensive care,' says Judith. 'Touch and go. As Derek said when I told him, it makes you wonder what Sally's legal position would be.'

'The number of children I know with a fatal nut allergy,' groans Cassie. 'I live in terror.'

She draws her sunglasses out of her bag and puts them on, but this does not prevent Judith from noticing the tears in her eyes.

'I'm a bit fed up,' explains Cassie. 'The doctor says he can't do anything about this trouble with my ears.'

'It's the colour of your downstairs,' says Judith without missing a beat. 'You should get my Feng Shui friend in. Anyone who has ear trouble, sinusitis, catarrh, that sort of thing, they should never have walls that colour.'

'What, magnolia?' says Cassie.

'Cream,' Judith corrects her. 'Dairy products. Milk. Cheese. Terribly mucilaginous. You should ring my Feng Shui friend. What have you got to lose?'

'This ringing noise, for a start,' says Cassie, smacking the side of her head, exasperated.

She spends the next couple of hours in the park pleasantly enough, watching the children and chatting to her friend, but not for one minute does she lose awareness of the minatory knife-sharpening noise inside her skull.

The official transition from afternoon to evening in Kew is marked at this time of year by the lighting of a thousand barbecues. This Saturday it is Cassie's neighbour's turn to host the road's annual summer party. The seasonal stench of paraffin and hickory-impregnated briquettes hangs low in the muggy air.

The women stand in clumps on the patio, sipping white wine and keeping an eye on the children, who surge around the forest their solid legs provide. The men have gravitated to the end of the garden under the trees where they help themselves to icy cans of lager from the turquoise cool-box standing on the picnic table.

Above them roars a steady stream of package flights and others. It is now at that point in the year when there are always three planes in the visible arch of the sky, lined up like formation gymnasts. Every forty seconds the barbecue guests fall silent without thinking at the peak of the central plane's trajectory, and then carry on as normal. Cassie remembers her first summer here and the way, inaudible through the din, people had mouthed at her like earnest goldfish: 'You don't even notice it after a while.'

She pours herself a third glass of wine and joins a group of women who are talking about what they are going to do on New Year's Eve. Carol has booked a family package to Paris, where it is rumoured the Eiffel Tower will lay a giant egg. Donna, recently divorced, hopes to fly to Tonga for a seafood feast on the night, if she can sort out the trouble with the Air Miles people; then on to Samoa. Christine is hoping to dodge across the dateline on Concorde so that she can see the new century dawn twice.

'I was just saying to Nigel the other day,' says Amanda from number twelve, 'Wouldn't it be nice to see the sun rise from Mount Kilimanjaro. But I don't know what we'd do with the children, nobody'll be wanting to babysit that night, will they?'

'I really don't see why air travel has to be so convenient

and cheap,' says Cassie. 'People should think twice before crossing the world.'

It is exactly as though she has not spoken. Nobody ever *listens* to me, she thinks.

'Frivolous and greedy,' she throws in for good measure.

'Amanda went down to Cornwall for the eclipse last week, didn't you Amanda,' says Donna. 'On that overnight train from Paddington, what was it called; champagne breakfast, the works.'

'The Fin de Siècle something or other,' says Amanda. 'Yes, it was a bit gloomy, the actual eclipse, but the rest of it was a really good laugh.'

'My God! Look at those ants!' cries Carol with a faint scream, having caught sight of the swarming insect mass pouring out from an airbrick. 'They've all grown wings!'

She runs off indoors for a kettle of boiling water while the rest of them crouch down to examine the glistening insect mass.

'They look a lot bigger than normal ants,' says Amanda.

'Probably from France,' says Donna. 'You know, like the Eurowasps. Double the size.'

'Oh, not Europe again,' says Amanda, tutting.

Cassie fills her glass and walks unsteadily off across the lawn towards the men. She has that sense of being able to see everything with perfect clarity, but nobody will listen to her.

The men are talking about whether the new century really only starts on the first of January 2001, as the spoilsport Swiss claim, and are speculating about how many work days will be lost, how long the celebrations and their hangovers will last.

'The good thing about the beginning of the year 2000,'

says Christine's husband Greg, 'is that January the first is a Saturday so everyone will have the Sunday and the Monday to recover, because of course the Monday will be a bank holiday.'

'By then there'll have been a tidal wave of computer crashes,' says Amanda's husband Nigel, with relish. 'It'll be the El Nino of I.T. I tell you, it's unbelievable, half these guys I see haven't even started to address the Y2K problem.'

'Heads in the sand,' nods Carol's husband Terry. 'We're talking global economic meltdown.'

'Worse than that,' says Cassie. 'A thousand times worse.'

'Steven not back from the Philippines yet?' asks Terry, acknowledging her presence.

'He's up there right at this moment,' sighs Cassie, pointing at the sky.

'Let's hope air traffic control has sorted itself out before next year,' Greg chuckles knowingly. 'Because it's set to be the busiest year in aviation history.' He rubs his hands together and grins. 'Just make sure you're not partying under the flight path on New Year's Eve. Take it from me.'

'They're saying there'll be record levels of suicide attempts on the thirty-first of December,' muses Greg. 'Seems a funny time to do it.'

'I reckon they're including the doom and gloom merchants in those statistics,' says Terry. 'Like the ones camping out in the Himalayas. I mean, you're going to look a right plonker when the end of the world *doesn't* come, aren't you, so the only logical thing then is to top yourself.'

'You can't afford to worry about these things,' says Greg. 'Listen, we're due a sunstorm next year, which is when the

US tracking system goes down. Completely useless. Perfect opportunity for a nuclear attack. Germ warfare. Let's hope the bad boys haven't figured *that* one out.'

He takes a big gulp of lager and shrugs.

'Too late,' says Cassie obscurely, mournfully. She knows anything she says now is mere babbling into the wind.

'Cheer up, Cassandra,' Terry chides. 'It may never happen.'

Cassie looks over to where her boys are laughing and playing.

'That's the trouble,' she insists. 'It will. Any minute now.'

On board British Airways flight 666 from Manila the air is exhausted after thirteen hours of being recycled. It has been in and out of every lung on board and is now damply laden with droplet infection.

Steven is grey-faced and crumbling with jet-lag. He rubs his eyes, his whole face, and the tired flesh moves back and forth in folds. Bloody wild goose chase, he says to himself, removing his glasses and rubbing his eyes till they creak. Now he is nearly home, and glad that it's a Saturday. He'll be able to catch up on sleep. There has been a child nearby who has been crying for much of the journey, troubled by a recurrence of the sinusitis contracted earlier in summer while on a transatlantic flight to Disneyland with his father, who is from Boston, then back to his mother, who is English but works in Hong Kong where she met and married his father. Although now they are divorced.

The weary pretty air hostess smiles at Steven with just that quality of sympathetic tenderness he wishes Cassie would show him more often.

'Would you like a drink, sir?'

As she searches her trolley for a miniature Glenfiddich, she thinks ahead to this evening when she and her husband must have sex. Her next set of IVF injections is due next week; she only hopes the airline won't mess her flights around again or that's another month wasted. She'll be forty-one in October, and she's been doing this job for twenty years.

The pilot meanwhile rubs his eyes and takes a message from air traffic control. This descent to Heathrow has become a regular white-knuckle ride since they reduced the distance between incoming aircraft to a mere mile. A little bit of a holding delay here to fit into the landing sequence, he says suavely into the microphone. The planes are stacked up now, and with all that confusion between West Drayton and Swanwick recently too, he can't remember feeling as jittery as this on a routine flight in his entire career.

The sky darkens like a tyrant's face, from ordinary pallor into deep fierce violet-grey. There is yellow lightning, the forked flicker of a monstrous snake's tongue, then a grandiloquent roll of thunder like the tattoo before an execution. Above the general steam and vapour scowls a rainbow arch of refracted brilliance.

The aircraft continue to follow the trajectory of this arch on their descent to Heathrow, and now they fly one after the other into an ominously gigantic boxer's ear of a cloud. Lost in this vaporous mass, British Airways flight 666 from Manila follows an instruction from the arrivals controller until it finds itself fifty feet vertically and a hundred feet horizontally from a Virgin Express Boeing 737 acting on a

71

contradictory instruction. Then both pilots become aware of the danger at the same time, and the incident almost becomes another near-miss for investigation by the Department of Transport. But not quite.

There is a noise like the crack of doom. The enormous cloud lights up as though targeted by a celestial flamethrower. Over in West Drayton a man in air traffic control has a heart attack which leads directly to the mid-air conflagration of a dozen more incoming flights.

Now aircraft like stingray are plunging, yellow eyes aglare, roaring and screaming as they explode into the glass houses at Kew Gardens and decimate the placid domestic streets surrounding. Steven joins his wife and children, but only in a manner of speaking. Piecemeal. Planes plough into the Hogarth roundabout at Chiswick and put an end to the permanent crawl of the South Circular. A row of double-fronted villas in Castelnau is flattened like a pack of cards, then rises in flames, joined by adjacent avenues of blazing red-brick houses. Mortlake is obliterated and Worple Way razed to the ground. East Sheen is utterly laid waste.

Fire consumes the sky and falls to earth in flaming comets and limbs and molten fragments of fuselage, where for two days and nights it will devour flesh and grass and much else besides in a terrible and unnatural firestorm for miles around south-west London.

And of course that – as Cassie would say were she still in one piece – *that* is only the beginning.

Burns and the Bankers

They were sitting down at last. There were over a thousand of them. All that breath and flesh meant the air beneath the chandeliers had very soon climbed to blood heat despite the dark sparkle of frost outside on Park Lane. An immense prosperous hum filled the hotel ballroom, as if all the worker bees of the British Isles were met to celebrate industriousness.

Nicola Beaumont used her tartan-ribboned menu to fan herself. The invitation had said six-thirty, so she had dashed straight from Ludgate Hill, having changed in literally two minutes in the Ladies, after a meeting with Counsel which had stretched out far too long; at the end of a day which had started with an eight o'clock meeting; with heels, earrings and lipstick going on in the back of the cab here; only to find that they were expected to stand around drinking alcohol for over an hour. And she'd somehow forgotten to prepare herself for the inevitable Caledonian overkill, all these sporrans and dirks and coy talk of the lassies.

Big Dougal was down from Edinburgh for the occasion, she'd noted, encircled by a servile coterie of younger men. She had been standing near enough to hear fragments of the incredibly circumlocutory anecdote with which he was, as he would no doubt have put it, regaling them. '. . . And that young gentleman, desirous of purchasing a property not a million miles away from the aforementioned office in Dumfries, then found himself embroiled in negotiations of a not entirely shall we say *salubrious* nature . . .'

Oh what windbags the Scots are, thought Nicola, she always forgot in between, but what blowhard old windbags they are really. Look at these young men smiling like stiff-necked nutcrackers, the ricti of servile mirth baring their teeth. It was a terrible thing, ambition; or, as Dougie would doubtless have put it, the desire for advancement. She herself had climbed the greasy pole a while back, she had been a full partner for six years now, so that slavish part of it was behind her, thank heavens; although of course the business of winning and pleasing clients was ongoing. That was why she was here now holding a tumbler of whisky – how she hated whisky, the stink of it, the rubbish they talked about it. But this was an important anniversary year for the Federation of Caledonian Bankers and they had decided to mark it by bringing together senior staff, clients and professional advisers for a mega-Burns Night.

She turned towards another group. Here, a lawyer she knew who had recently been made a partner at Clarence Sweets was talking to the head leasing partner at Iddon Featherstone, each with a black-tied husband at her elbow.

'But is he good with them at weekends?' the Clarence Sweets woman was eagerly demanding. 'Hands on, I mean.'

'Oh yes, he takes them swimming,' said the head leasing partner. 'Out on their bikes.' She shrugged. 'Though of course he's usually working at weekends.'

The husbands under discussion gazed into their tumblers of whisky like wordless children. Each of the four standing there had that day crammed twelve hours' worth of work into ten in order to attend this banquet, and the whisky was hitting stomachs which had long since forgotten the snatched midday sandwich.'

No, I do not want to compare nightmare journey times to the Suzuki session, thought Nicola, whose four-year-old twins went to the same violin teacher as the Clarence Sweets woman's daughter, somewhere out in Surrey, every Saturday. She scanned the packed room and caught sight of her husband Charlie on the other side, arriving late. He was looking stockier than ever. All that flying he'd had to do in the last year hadn't helped, she thought; six or seven times a month recently, including Japan and Australia. Not good for the waistline. Not good for the heart.

By the time she'd threaded her way across through the crowd, Torquil Cameron had got his mitts on Charlie. That was sharp of him, to remember him from Goodwood.

'A-*ha*,' smiled Torquil above his frilly jabot, then he bowed from the hips in that way men do in kilts, the better to show off his pleats, the swing of them. 'Delighted you could be here, Nicola. As you can see I've located your other half for you. Now I don't think you've met my own good lady wife, Jean.' Jean stood by him, the colour of a brick, free of make-up, in her fifties and a girlish white ballgown with a plaid sash athwart her bosom. She smiled at Nicola, who was wearing a black crêpe trousersuit, and her eyes showed disapproval mixed with shyness and fear.

'So, Nicola!' boomed Torquil. 'When was it exactly, the last time we had the pleasure of seeing you up in Auld Reekie?'

'Oh, not long ago, I think,' smiled Nicola, wondering why he had to be so ponderous. 'It was October, wasn't it? There was that day of meetings about the Yellow Target business. You took us all out for a good lunch at the Witchery, I seem to remember.'

'That's right, that's right!' crowed Torquil as though delighted and relieved. He turned to Charlie. 'You'll be looking forward to your haggis then?' he enquired. Charlie smiled wanly.

Following this welcome there had been an interminable stretch of time during which the thousand guests drifted slow as plankton past the seating plan and from there down the huge staircase into the ballroom.

'The things I do for you,' Charlie had muttered as they shuffled down the stairs.

'I sat through *Die* mostincrediblyboringold *Meistersingers* only last week for your lot,' she had reminded him. 'Four hours.'

'This'll be longer.'

'And *Orfeo and Eurydice* the week before.'

'That was *short*.'

'You'll be all right,' she had said crossly. 'Lots of whisky.'

'Did Harry make it into the team, d'you know?'

'As a reserve.'

Charlie had given a vexed snort.

'That boy. He's perfectly capable of it. He just doesn't try.'

'He said he missed the shot which would have got him a place. Just bad luck. He's very disappointed.'

'So he should be.'

Their lives were both so busy that times of idleness alone together like this, on the staircase in a queue, were few and far between. They had over the years developed a breezy shorthand for talking about their four children, for exchanging vital information and intimate views as economically as possible, rather like a couple of fighter pilots crewing the same Mosquito.

Nicola had an extraordinarily retentive memory, which was invaluable not only in the practice of law but also at this sort of event, as she could memorise the seating plan and prime herself to ask the right questions about the various sporting activities and children of the clients involved. She was excellent on names and faces. So, as she and Charlie had made their slow way down, her mental picture had been as follows:

Susan Buchanan
Stay-at-home. Winsome.
Vegetarian. Three boys
under six.

Brian Mahon
Fifty-something. In Structured
Finance at Bank of Hibernia.
Tennis, squash.
Originally Belfast.
Heavy drinker.
Nice eyes.

Charlie Beaumont
Senior executive at
Schnell-Darwittersbank.
Mustn't get too drunk,
please.

Lily Forfar
Unknown quantity.

Deborah Mahon
Three girls, all grown up.
Hospital visiting. Bridge.
Ealing. Portugal.

Iain Buchanan
Glaswegian *émigré*.
London branch of Bank of
Alba. Lanky, hyper. Golf,
football, supports Partick
Thistle (cue football banter).
Heavy drinker.

Donald Forfar
Unknown quantity.
Doing well in the
heavy-hitting Edinburgh
branch of Bank of Alba.
Possible future work here;
currently with Clarence
Sweets but they
messed up a big case
for him last year.
Golf?

Nicola Beaumont
Partner at Littleboy & Pringle.

77

The table was bristling with slim silver vases of orchids and bottles of wine standing ready uncorked before forests of glasses and napkins pleated into white cockades and even little silver-plated quaichs, one each engraved with a guest's name, the date and the crest of the Caledonian Banking Federation.

'Well, Iain,' said Nicola to the man seated on her left. 'This is all very impressive.'

'And it hasn't even started yet,' said Iain. 'Here, let me pour you a glass. White or red? Have you been to a Burns Night before? No, well, there are a lot of speeches I can warn you, so you'll be glad of a glass in front of you.'

'Cheers,' said Nicola, who knew this man slightly and liked him, his sharpness and frankness.

'*Slanjiva*,' he replied, or something like it.

She was aware of Donald Forfar on her right, a strong thick-set presence, the sort of build that looked good in a kilt. Whereas tall lean men like Iain Buchanan were far better off in jeans. She was about to turn and introduce herself but then Iain was tapping her arm.

'Here's Torquil Cameron now,' he said, directing her gaze towards the top table on its platform hundreds of metres away from them. 'He'll be giving the welcome and he'll take his time because he's a big balloon, but then he'll say grace and we can all get started.'

'Oh good,' said Nicola.

It was very hot. She picked up the menu to fan herself, and her mind stretched back through the packed day. Every minute had been spoken for. Her chargeable hours were on target so far this year but it was a constant battle. She hadn't managed a full half-hour with the children this morning; it couldn't be helped but it made her feel a bit sick considering she was out tonight again for the second time this week and it was only Wednesday. Jade was so sarcastic these days but she liked the benefits, the good school, the nice holidays. She, Nicola, would make up that twenty-minute shortfall, she would squeeze it in somehow tomorrow.

She took a sip of wine and immediately the alcohol rose up behind her face to somewhere at eyebrow level and she thought, that's hit the spot. The one thing all us hard-working and often successful people can't have, she realised as she gazed around her at the sea of heated faces, is TIME. She took another sip and felt a number of tiny muscles in her shoulders relax like a sigh. That's it, she decided. Water from now on or I'll never last.

It made her crisp with irritation, that she could have arrived half an hour later and no harm done. But that's the deal, she reminded herself. She had always to be thinking ahead. That was what she had to do. She was unable to sit inside the minute; it was a joke in their family that she couldn't sit still. She had a beautiful house and she was never in it. She knew what the children were doing at every hour of the day, and she wasn't there. She kept it all up in the air, she never lost her grip. So much so that it would be positively dangerous for her to relax. If she were to let go it didn't bear thinking about, the fall-out.

The waiters were moving in massed ranks across the floor, bearing soup to the tables while Torquil Cameron carried on. He was paying lip service to Burns now.

'And where, ladies and gentlemen,' boomed Torquil Cameron, 'Where would we be without poetry?'

Nicola caught Charlie's eye across the table and smothered a giggle. She glanced at other faces and saw the pained expressions of piety, as though God had been mentioned, or cancer.

The moment passed. Poetry! thought Nicola. That's all we need. Doubtless some Scot would start spouting Burns later and it was in dialect if she remembered rightly. Wee sleekit cowrin timrous beastie. As the man boomed on, she became aware of an unfamiliar feeling: boredom. Of course one ought to be able to make these dead patches of time work for one. She had friends who recommended meditation techniques for just such occasions. Om, wasn't it. Or was it visualise a beach. Which reminded her, she *must* get that cheque off to Better Villas asap.

At last the big balloon had finished. Now he was announcing grace, and they all had to bow their heads over their soup bowls.

> Some hae meat that canna eat,
> And some wad eat that want it;
> But we hae meat, and we can eat,
> And sae the Lord be thankit.

Then the hubbub started up again and there was the chinking of a thousand spoons as they tackled their Cullen Skink.

Nicola glanced around their table. She realised with relief that, so great was the noise, she would not be obliged to talk to anyone beyond Iain Buchanan on her left and this other man on her right. Iain's wife Susan, directly opposite, was giving Charlie the sparrow's bright look askance, while he smiled falsely back. Susan was smart and chirpy, as Nicola remembered, but not very deep. Also she was a full-time mother of the sort who drew their skirts away when Nicola approached, while exuding a neediness to freeze the cockles of your heart. Iain on her left was working all the hours of the day and night, Nicola happened to know, as he badly wanted to be made deputy head of the branch, and that move was still a good year off.

On the other side of Charlie was Deborah Mahon, a vaguely smiling woman of fifty-five or fifty-six, who had not earned any money for over thirty years. She had had a front-of-house job in the bank for a little while before she got married, back in the mists of time, when she was still in her decorative early twenties, and since then had stayed indoors to look after her husband and three demanding, confident and ambitious daughters, the youngest of whom had just started university.

Nicola knew how the talk went at this kind of mixed do with spouses. The men would address the women beside them with bored chivalry, feeding them brief obvious questions about their children or their house or their little part-time jobs and then the women would chat on, working away at keeping the conversational bonfire alight, pulling more than their weight in an exchange which really was nineteen to the dozen. But she herself was not one of these women. She had a foot in both camps. Not only had she borne four children but she also earned as much as her husband and more than Iain Buchanan. So she would be able to talk with the men about money and the new Japanese restaurant near Gracechurch Street and – barring sport, of course – things that really interested them. Still she wore high heels and earrings and noticed that this man on her right, Donald Forfar, was quite appealing in a solid saturnine sort of way.

'"The Selkirk Grace",' he said, waving his soup spoon at

her. 'So called because Robert Burns repeated those lines when he dined with the Earl of Selkirk. Although the fact of the matter is, he didn't write them, they were around well before he was born and were known as "The Covenanter's Grace".'

'How interesting,' said Nicola; and then, in case that sounded satirical, 'I love Scotland but I've never been to Selkirk,' which was inane but somehow less hostile.

'Unfortunately my wife has just gone down with the flu,' said Donald Forfar, when Nicola enquired about her absence. She herself never got ill. Apart from three months' maternity leave around each of her labours, she had never taken a day off sick. Touch wood.

It turned out that Donald was a fan of Robert Burns. He was reading a new biography of Burns at the moment.

'Oh dear,' said Nicola, whose busy life did not allow for this although she always read at least two books when they went away on holiday and one of her New Year's resolutions had been to join a Book Club. 'I really must read more.'

'But as a pleasure,' smiled Donald. 'You make it sound like a duty.'

Yes well, thought Nicola. The packed quality of her life meant that it was physically, mentally, impossible for her to sit inside the minute like a thin-skinned raindrop proud on a nasturtium leaf, impossible for her to sit still and read a book. Her nights were necessarily short and her sleep was a dreamless passing out. No drowsing in the morning was possible, ever.

Iain Buchanan was leaning forwards now to talk to Donald Forfar.

'That's right, we moved six months ago,' he was saying. 'It's a mansion, so I've heard,' said Donald Forfar. 'Acres of green sward.'

'Och, it's nice for Susan and the boys to have a bit of a garden to run around in,' said Iain. 'They love the tennis court. Talking of which. You know Roderick MacKenzie? Excuse me, Nicola. Perhaps you know him too? Investments at the Lombard Street branch of the Bank of Auld Scotia?'

'Married to Lucy MacKenzie over at Leviathan?'

'That's the one. Dropped down dead during a game of tennis, the day after Boxing Day. Heart attack.'

'Yes. Four children. Shocking.'

'He was from Aberdeen originally, wasn't he?'

'I thought she was Irish.'

'No, no, she's English. Very English.'

'And what is this?' said Brian Mahon, leaning across the space left by Donald Forfar's absent wife, peering across Iain Buchanan and joining in. 'Are we now reduced to comparing the English, the Irish and the Scots? Is that the game?' He looked fairly drunk already, his colour high and his eyes blue as the sea.

'Donald was just saying how industrious us Scots are compared to the feckless feckin Irish,' said Iain. 'And how we carry our drink better too.'

'Don't listen to them, now, Nicola,' said Brian, turning his dark-fringed blue gaze on her. 'We have the better poetry and music. What's Burns to Yeats?'

'We've got Shakespeare,' said Nicola, but they ignored her.

'The Irish,' said Iain. 'Not to put too fine a point on it, are no so gifted in the intellectual department.'

'The Scots are always thinking of number one, Nicola,' said Brian. 'It's impossible for a Scotsman to fall in love.'

'Och aye, that describes Robert Burns perfectly,' hooted Iain.

'Nature over nurture,' mused Donald Forfar. It was rather sweet, thought Nicola, the way he spoke like a schoolmaster. 'He was steeped in the disciplines of survival and repression,' he continued, 'but still the poetry in him triumphed.'

'Education,' declared Iain, swirling his whisky glass then sniffing it. 'Application. They're the reason why Scotland's best.'

At the mention of education, Nicola began to salivate like Pavlov's dog, and was just preparing to quiz these men about the schools their children attended when she was deflected by Brian Mahon.

'Scots on the make,' he scoffed. 'That's what they do, Nicola, they emigrate as soon as they can in order to better themselves, even if it's only down south to Guildford like Iain here, then they lecture anyone who'll bear it on the virtues of the auld country.'

'Of course Scotland stayed with the traditional teaching methods at the time England abandoned them,' mused Donald Forfar. 'And the presence of an educated working class has meant we have a more genuinely democratic society than the English in consequence.'

'Donald went to Fettes,' said Iain Buchanan drily.

'Oh, *Fettes!*' said Nicola, riveted.

Before she could cross-question him about old school-mates, however, she was interrupted by someone in a kilt shouting for them all to stand for the arrival of the haggis. She glanced at her watch during the general upheaval this

84

involved. Gone nine. The twins would have been asleep for over an hour. Then there was an awful whining noise as a piper threaded his way through the tables, followed by a chef carrying something beige on a silver plate, then a third play actor holding a bottle of whisky aloft in each hand. These three certainly took their time, apparently pacing themselves by the slow handclap that accompanied them to the top table.

'Will you look there, Donald,' said Iain Buchanan, craning to see the hefty old Scot rising to his feet on the top table's dais as the rest of the room sat down again. 'It's old Shoogie Henderson who'll be giving the address to the haggis. He was in with the bricks right enough. When's he due to retire, d'you think?'

'He's past sixty,' said Donald, pouring whisky into the little silver quaichs and passing them round the table.

'That's the trouble with this organisation,' fumed Iain, tipping the contents of his quaich into his mouth. 'Nae movement. Blocked at the top.'

'I prefer the Tamdhu,' said Donald. 'The Speyside malt is softer.'

Iain's face was redder than it had been an hour ago. He held his quaich out for a refill. He was at that crucial age, somewhere around thirty-seven or thirty-eight, when his work life must either take off very soon with the rocket fuel of promotion and increased power, or stick for good in a rut until retirement age.

Up at the crackling microphone Shoogie Henderson cleared his resented old throat, and some sort of hush crept by degrees across the huge room. Then, in the manner of Father Christmas, he read:

Fair fa' your honest, sonsie face,
Great Chieftan o'the Puddin-race!
Aboon them a' ye tak your place,
  Painch, tripe, or thairm:
Weel are ye worthy of a grace
  As lang's my airm.

And it was as lang as his airm, too. On and on it went, incomprehensible to Nicola, and smug and ridiculous.

'His knife see Rustic-labour dight,' continued old Shoogie with relish, 'An' cut you up wi' ready slight . . .'

He paused and smiled at the kilted loon beside him, who seized a knife and plunged it histrionically into the haggis. A cheer went up.

'What exactly is in it?' asked Nicola, as a plate of tweedy brownish morsels was placed in front of her.

'Och, it's just a sausage,' said Donald, brushing her arm as he reached for the whisky. 'But they use the stomach bag as casing rather than the more usual intestinal tubing.'

'But what's *in* it?' said Nicola, meeting his eyes, which were like black glass and slightly hooded. 'I want to know what it's made of.'

'The liver, lights and windpipe of a sheep,' said Donald, glittering at her.

'Right,' said Nicola. 'Thank you.'

'Over here with the tatties and neeps,' Iain Buchanan sang out to a waiter.

On every table Nicola could see men in kilts smacking their lips and going for seconds. She tasted a scrap of haggis and found it both mealy and salty. An ocean of alcohol was being drained in nips and sips and gulps, in a steamingly hot room on a thousand empty stomachs. Faces were red and damp, and drastically split with laughter. The noise was tremendous. It was almost ten o'clock, Nicola saw with another covert glance at her watch, and they weren't even on the main course, the haggis being in the nature of an entrée as far she could tell.

'Here we are, Nicola,' said Iain Buchanan as a bevy of Scottish country dancers trooped onto the raised square platform in the middle of the room. 'Here comes the heedrum hodrum. Listen out for the noise they make. One or the other of them will give a wee hooch now and then to show their particular enjoyment.'

'I've not seen dancing at a Burns Supper before,' mused Donald. 'It's obviously no expense spared tonight.'

The young dancers were a sad, odd-looking crew, and the platform shook as they leaped and jumped. Hi-yeuch! they went in a scrubbed desperate way, baring their teeth brightly and panting. It was almost as sexless as Irish dancing, thought Nicola, with the upper body having nothing to do with the rest, as if some radical divorce went on at hip level. She looked around her. All this archness and stiffness and verbosity! You shuddered to think of bedtime.

She eyed her table, which had temporarily given up on conversation because of the heedrum hodrum, and considered the men. Charlie was still a main contender, though he must have put on twenty pounds since the summer. Iain wasn't bad-looking but for some reason he came nowhere. Tolerable, she smiled to herself, but not handsome enough to tempt *me*. Brian Mahon now, although well into his fifties, was obviously still interested, whereas his wife, just as obviously, had the dusty look of one who has no desires of her own. No, it would have to be this man Donald Forfar, he was definitely the favourite, although his thick black hair looked worryingly turfy. She was fascinated by the way the shadow on his jaw was growing darker as the evening progressed. At this rate he'd have a beard by midnight. He had drawn his chair out a little in order to watch the dancing and Nicola was able to steal a look at his stout calves in their woolly knee socks, and at his big bare knees.

The meal dragged on, through warm sliced meat then some sort of muesli concoction until at last they reached the coffee stage. Not long now, thought Nicola, unwrapping a mint. It was a nasty shock, then, when Donald, turning a genial eye upon her, declared, 'Now at last the evening proper can begin!'

'But that business before the haggis,' faltered Nicola, 'that poem, wasn't that *it?*'

'No, no,' laughed Donald. 'The heart of a Burns Night is the Immortal Memory. Someone has to make a speech in praise of Burns, and that's what it's called – the Immortal Memory.'

'Look who's giving it tonight,' crowed Brian Mahon from further up the table. 'It's Rory McCrindle. Have you seen his place in Farnham? Tartan sofas, tartan carpets, views of the heather-covered highlands. It's like Rob Roy's Cave.'

'Nothing to Iain's mansion in Guildford, so I've been told,' said Donald. 'I hear it has a swimming pool, Iain; am I right?'

I'm not sure I'll be able to last through this, thought Nicola. I've had enough. Across the table, Charlie winked at her. He looked red and pie-eyed. A few minutes earlier she had heard him ask their waiter for more walt misky. No help from that quarter, she thought, wondering how she would get him home.

'And this Immortal Memory event,' said Nicola. 'Roughly how, er, *long* does it tend to go on?'

'Och, the Immortal Memory is only the start of it,' said Iain. 'Don't worry. You'll love it.'

'The Immortal Memory is a moral dose of salts,' said Donald. 'Once a year you listen to the story of Burns' life and poetry, then you examine your own life in the light of his. It's an improving speech, Nicola.'

'So he's like a saint?' said Nicola.

'Not exactly a saint,' said Donald.

'A man's a man for a' that,' burst in Iain.

'The social, friendly, honest man,' rolled out Donald, 'Whate'er he be.'

'For a' that,' said Iain again.

'Yes, the English all know bits of Shakespeare,' said Nicola. 'To be or not to be, is this a dagger that I see before me. But we don't try to copy his life, leaving Anne Hathaway in the lurch. With twins, too.'

'Oor Rab had mair twins than Shakespeare,' said Iain aggressively. 'He had them coming oot his ears.'

'No, Nicola, it's the litany of his life which has taken hold,' said Donald. 'Barefoot, boxbed, homespun, peat fires by which he listened to Old Betty's ghost stories, hard labour on father's failing farm from age of seven. They were poor but they were happy. See "The Cotter's Saturday Night" which is the great Scottish Family Values poem.'

'Aye one for the lassies, but,' said Iain.

'Oh, aye one for the lassies,' agreed Donald with a nasal whine of mock-disapprobation. 'Enough babies fathered to get him denounced from the kirk pulpit and make him consider sailing for Jamaica . . . But in the nick of time a publisher takes up his collection of dialect poems and they are a huge hit with everyone buying them from the crême de la crême of Edinburgh society . . .'

'Like your good self, Donald,' remarked Iain.

'. . . From the literati in Edinburgh to the farm labourers and maidservants for miles around,' continued Donald mildly. 'Highland Mary dies in childbirth, his wean of course . . .'

'But he married Bonny Jean thingwy, right enough,' said Iain.

'Yes, he marries faithful Jean Armour, mother of nine of his children . . .'

'Oh, that's why the pudding was called Jean's Brose,' interrupted Nicola. 'That muesli thing.'

'. . . Fails at farming, gets a job as an exciseman, gets ill,' continued Donald. 'Dies aged thirty-seven.'

'Thirty-seven!' exclaimed Nicola. 'Shakespeare was over fifty.'

'Burns had more *twins*, though,' insisted Iain.

'Not only that, Nicola,' Donald continued, 'But the Immortal Memory will be built round one of several well-worn themes.'

'Burns Mark One,' cut in Iain. 'The Ploughman Poet.'

'"To a mountain daisy, on turning one down with a plough",' said Donald. 'Burns Mark Two, the Lover. Aye one for the lassies, heh heh. O my luve's like a red red rose. Burns Mark Three, the convivial man . . .'

'. . . Burns was nae an alkie,' glossed Iain. 'Enjoyed a wee dram with his friends but did not get regularly paralettic.'

'We are na fou, we're nae that fou,' quoted Donald.

'And so on,' said Iain with an air of resignation, pouring more whisky. 'But look, McCrindle's on his way up to the microphone.'

It was not really possible to see the man, so far away was the top table. He was a tartan ant in a tartan formicary.

'Of course, Burns was – not to put too fine a point on it – a *peasant*,' came his amplified voice.

'Burns Mark One,' hissed Donald and Iain each side of her, one in each ear.

She turned off, as she did when she had to sit through an opera. She decided to regard this as relaxation time. Looking across the table at Charlie she felt relief again at not having to talk to the wives. She knew their type, particularly Brian Mahon's wife, the older one, whose eye she caught for a moment before looking away. Oh yes, that one had a look that said, 'You, with your four-wheel drive and your greedy ways. I don't know why you bother to have children if you don't look after them.'

She tuned into Rory McCrindle to see how it was going.

'As teenagers Burns and his young friends formed a club, the Tarbolton Bachelors,' he announced with laborious pleasure. 'The rules laying down no admittance to snobs – here I quote – "*and especially no mean-spirited, worldly mortal, whose only will is to heap up money*".'

A ripple of laughter swept through the room like a gust of wind in a barleyfield.

'*Why is the bard unfitted for the world,*' he continued, '*yet has so keen a relish of its pleasures?*'

Well, quite, thought Nicola. Absolutely. There was her daughter Jade insisting that she didn't want a life like hers,

but where did she think it all came from? Her latest talk
was of being an events organiser, of how she was going to
have a portfolio career and lots of fun. Just to irritate
Nicola (Nicola felt sure) she wore a T-shirt with a slogan
across her breasts – "ALL OF THIS and my dad's loaded
too". Would she really rather be like that woman, Brian
Mahon's wife, whose high point of the year was probably
masterminding her fifties-style turkey-and-sprouts family
Christmas? Whereas she, Nicola, had been able to deal
with the festive season by sweeping the whole lot off to
Lapland. Granted it had been a nightmare to pack for with
the nanny back off to Sheffield on Christmas Eve, then
Chloe had broken the little finger on her left hand slipping
on a patch of ice at Rovaniemi airport, but still it had been
amazing. All that snow, and the children had adored the
sleigh ride with Santa's elves.

Now he was quoting from one of the ploughman poet's
letters. '*If miry ridges and dirty dunghills are to engross the best part
of my soul immortal, I had better been a rook or a magpie and then I
should not have been plagued with any ideas superior to the breaking of
clods and picking up of grubs.*'

Home was a wasteland during the week anyway as she'd
discovered during her maternity leaves, just nannies or
women like Deborah Mahon for company. Your eyes went
dull inside three days, your thighs turned to Turkish
Delight, you put on half a stone a week. She loved her
children more than life itself (forced as one was into
Goneril-and-Regan hyperbole), and so did Charlie in his
way; but, like him, she preferred to subcontract out much
of the work of parenthood. She had a wonderful nanny,
worth her weight in gold, she'd had her for four years now
and dreaded to think what would happen when she left.

Burns was exchanging the dirty dunghills of Mossgiel for lionisation in the drawing rooms of Edinburgh, where his delight in educated talk sat painfully alongside his contempt for hereditary privilege. She could feel it all around her, history, these chaps, their wives, waiting to drive her back indoors. But, like Burns in the Edinburgh drawing rooms, she would not be intimidated; she had considered her position and thought out where she stood on this one.

When Nicola was a child, her mother had existed in a maroon cloud of rage and frustration. If ever the guilt-wagon comes within five miles of me now, she thought, I remember that cloud and shout with relief. She hadn't exactly been born with a silver spoon in her mouth but the eleven plus had allowed her into the game. She had stretched and competed and done well. Minutes became meaningful units, hours added up to something. Then came the children and working for a partnership, and all her time management skills had come into their own.

Sometimes the stay-at-home mothers tried to pick her brains about the best schools for their daughters. Why bother? she wanted to say, Why bother flogging them over exam hurdles if your girls are going to end up like you, sipping coffee in between school runs? And of course there were no men at home during the days – they sped off early to be where the action was. To work. To make money.

Rory McCrindle was winding up his Immortal Memory with a few lofty homiletic insights. 'That human decency and human worth have for the most part their dwelling among the poor he had a perception more constant, more pressing and more experienced than any other man of his epoch,' he intoned.

I don't buy that old idea of poverty being a virtue,

thought Nicola. What's *wrong* with money? Money's good for people. That she should earn her living had been an article of faith. She hadn't slaved at her exams and said no to fun for all those years of torts and statutes, just for something to pass the time until she started a family. What a waste of government money, for a start. And she couldn't take a couple of years off. *No.* She'd be dead in the water. She wouldn't be allowed back in.

Also, they *needed* her money. It would be too dangerous to rely on Charlie's income alone with job security as it was. It took an incredible amount to keep the show on the road, what with the mortgage and childcare, not to mention Charlie's alimony payments to the dreaded Joanne. She felt many years old for an instant, a hard-worked horse. 'Driven' was the adjective that had always been applied to her, usually as a compliment, but –

Her thoughts were interrupted by a sudden pandemonium of scraping chairs and shouts of 'Rabbie!' and 'Rabbie Burns!' as all around her people rose to their feet, tossing back the contents of their quaichs with stagey bravado. An emotional wave of applause followed. These hard-working cautious bankers and their like had been moved to the edge of tears by this account, familiar to them all, of the poet's reckless, penurious life and of his death made fearful by the terror of debt.

'I hear there was a fair bit of trouble over planning the speeches,' said Donald, sipping his way towards incaution. 'Apparently Alistair Wallace, he's the head of the Aberdeen branch, well he was the obvious choice to give the Toast to the Lassies.'

'Toast to the *Lassies*?' said Nicola disdainfully.

'Yes, the Toast to the Lassies usually comes directly after the Immortal Memory, but because of the numbers involved tonight they have to take things a wee bit slower to allow for the food to be served and taken away and so on.'

'Why Alistair Wallace?' asked Iain. 'Why not a younger man? Though *most* of us are younger than Alistair Wallace. It wouldnae be difficult to be younger than Alistair Wallace.'

'His Toast to the Lassies has been in demand with Burns Societies all along the East Coast for the past thirty years,' said Donald. 'He's a local hero. But when it finally came to the run-through down in London, much to everybody's dismay his famous speech was obviously impossible. Offensive. Sexist.'

'Oh, not that P.C. stuff again,' said Iain in disgust.

'You could see where the problem lay,' brooded Donald. 'Your average traditional Burns Supper, it's nearly all men that go along. The wives stay at home. It's a wee bit Masonic, if you like. And of course the organiser of this big Caledonian Federation anniversary event realised in the nick of time that mibbe half the guests here tonight were likely to be female. Things would have to be updated.'

'So what did they do?' asked Nicola, intrigued despite herself. She loved management issues.

'Well, they couldn't drop Alistair altogether, that would have been offensive too. He'd never have understood, and neither would his fans. So they decided to shunt him into a less controversial slot, the Reply to the Immortal Memory. That's usually just a brief vote of thanks if it's included at all. And he was requested to keep the obscenities to a minimum.'

'Oh great,' said Iain angrily. 'The classic sense-of-humour failure. That's great.'

'Not when you think about it,' Donald demurred. 'You can see their point. It would have been like asking an audience where half the guests were black to sit and laugh at racist jokes. You wouldn't call that a sense-of-humour failure.'

'That's different,' growled Iain. 'Anyway, who *will* be giving the Toast to the Lassies now?'

'They found an academic with an interest in Scottish Literature,' shrugged Donald. 'Birkbeck College, I think it was.'

'Oh how super, an *academic*,' said Iain. 'Are they bringing back that Talisker then?'

'Is this the man who's been causing all the trouble?' asked Nicola.

'The very one,' said Donald, craning his neck towards the top table.

This controversial old speaker Alistair Wallace rattled out anecdotes in thick hawking gutturals. Nicola's ears took in about half of what he said, while for the rest of it she sat with the strained expression of one who is hard of hearing. I can't believe the time, she thought; we're never going to be allowed home. His voice was like artillery, and his tone was brutal, laconic, almost East European she decided; although there was also something purely Scottish in its blend of romantic stoicism. As far as she could tell, his speech had had nothing at all to do with Burns. At least it didn't go on as long as the one before. Now it was drawing to a close with a joke for the bankers.

'"Och, this way of life is all fine and dandy," says Angus

to his friend Gavin. "The money's fine, the job's great, but I find the stress is getting to me. I get that hyped up sometimes I don't know what to do with myself."

"'You know fine well that's an occupational hazard in jobs like ours, big hitters in the City," says Gavin. "Big swinging dicks as we are. I'll tell you what I do when I get that way myself, when I get stressed out. When I get like that, first opportunity occurs, I drive back to my house, kiss the wife at the front door, take her upstairs to the bedroom. And half an hour later I'm right as rain. Feeling like a million dollars. Ready to get back into the fray. You should try it."

"'Well," says Angus. "Thanks for the tip. It certainly seems to work for you.'"

The men were sniggering quietly over their whisky. Susan Buchanan had her head cocked on one side to listen, like a bright-eyed sparrow, while Deborah Mahon had assumed her vague all-purpose smile. Nicola regarded the grin on her husband's tired grey face. Charlie was still her darling, but he wasn't exactly Young Lochinvar any more.

'A week later,' the speaker continued, 'Angus and Gavin meet again. "You're looking much better, Angus," cries Gavin. "You're looking years younger, relaxed, not a care in the world." "Thanks to you," smiles Angus. "I took your advice. Next time I felt stressed out I drove back to the house. Knocked at the door. Kissed the wife. Took her upstairs to the bedroom. Half an hour later, right as rain. Just as you said. She was a bit surprised at first, your good lady, but after I explained it was you that had sent me round she was fine about it.'"

The enormous room erupted. All around, hot red faces

were disintegrating into guffaws and whinnying. Nicola smiled politely and felt a shudder run through her.

Stress! She could handle it. She positively enjoyed jumping in its salty waves. The danger was, you got *too* good at it. You started to see time that was not paid time – chargeable hours – as dead time; unprofitable; unless it was directly recuperative – the gym, for example, twice a week to keep up this level of energy – servicing the machine. There was of course another rhythm, the rhythm of children and old people, being patient, watching the grass grow; but she couldn't see herself doing that for another thirty years at least. She didn't *want* to take it easy. She was young, or at least in the prime of life; she loved stirring productive movement. Stillness just didn't do it for her.

And why is it always down to me, thought Nicola, this talk of having it all and so on? I took the top first in my year. I'm cleverer than him though I don't rub it in. We have four children. But there's no question of him adapting his hours to the family or helping manage the nanny and the house and all that *that* involves. There is never for one moment a suggestion that Charlie should budge.

To be fair, he never suggested she stop working either.

'Iain, it's gone eleven,' said Nicola. 'I don't want to sound rude but I'm wondering about the babysitter.'

'There's a way to go yet. You can't hurry a Burns Night. You shouldnae worry, your sitter will be fine, she'll be asleep in front of the telly.'

'It's true,' said Donald. 'There is no getting round it. You might as well enjoy it. Would you like another glass?'

'No thank you,' said Nicola, not smiling.

She must be the only person in the room who wasn't

drunk. How much more of this Burns stuff could there possibly be?

'Here we are, Nicola,' said Iain. 'Here's the Toast to the Lassies about to start. Here's the *academic*. Now we're in for a treat.'

As it happened, this next speech was so direct and affecting that Nicola found herself listening with all her attention for the first time.

The poet's mother Agnes had been the eldest of six, and when she was ten her mother had died, first telling Agnes that she must look after her little brothers and sisters. Not much later Agnes was courted by a ploughman, the two of them working daily together in the fields; but then, after seven years of this, she found him with another woman and finished with him. On the rebound she married William Burns, a tenant-farmer years older than herself. Their eldest son Robert did not inherit his mother's strict ideal of fidelity. He described himself as having a tinder heart always alight for some girl or other.

Famously there was Highland Mary, Mary Campbell, with whom he joined hands under the current of the brook where they met in a private marriage pledge, and who died in childbirth with his baby about the time Jean Armour was having his twins. Then there was May Cameron, a servant girl, and Jenny Clow, and Agnes McLehose (his Clarinda) in Edinburgh, and Anna Park, barmaid at the Dumfries Globe, who bore his daughter Betty nine days before Jean presented him with his third son.

Thank God I live in an age of contraception, thought Nicola. Of all the blessings of the modern world, that must be the greatest.

It was Jean Armour he eventually married, banishing

thoughts of the intellectual disparity between them in a stoutly worded letter – '*A wife's head is immaterial compared with her heart. My Jean has the kindest heart in the county, gratefully devoted with all its powers to love me. Indeed the poor girl has the most sacred enthusiasm for me and has not a wish but to gratify my every idea of her deportment.*' She bore nine of his children, four of whom died. '*Of the four children she bore me in seventeen months, two sets of twins, my eldest boy only is living,*' he wrote to a friend in 1788. '*But I reckon a twelve brace of children against I celebrate my twelfth wedding day – twenty-four christenings, twenty-four useful members of society! I am so enamoured of her prolific twin-bearing merit that I have given her the legal title which I now avow to the world.*'

There was something rather fab about having had the twins at forty, thought Nicola; bringing in new life when others that age were starting to worry about death. And she still wasn't too old, there was still just about time to squeeze in one last baby if she really felt like it.

Once Burns had married Jean Armour, he arranged for the babies he continued to father by other women to go to her rather than to his mother as before. 'Oor Rab could hae done wi' twa' wives,' Jean commented. On the day of his funeral, she gave birth to their ninth baby, a boy. She was left with five sons and little Betty Park. She was to live on for another thirty-eight years, two more of her sons dying early during that time.

'In his own time Burns was criticised for immorality,' concluded the speaker. 'He wrote,

> O ye douce folk that live by rule
> Grave, tideless-blooded, calm an' cool

Your hearts are like a standing pool
Yc *never* stray . . .

That sort of love, the sort that moved Burns to poetry, it's like the sea. It ebbs and flows. It doesn't last. What remains when it's over? Why, the poetry of course. And the babies.'

'Oh dear,' said Nicola to Iain, wiping her eyes, while the applause died down around them. 'That was sad. That poor woman Jean.'

'Och aye, bonnie Jean,' said Iain. 'These days she'd have been a teleworker for the bank, right enough.'

'More security in that than in farming,' said Nicola.

'Security. Babies. I don't know.' Iain shook his head and poured more whisky. 'I'm no being rude, Nicola, but can I ask you something? Why do you have *four*? We've got the three and that's as much as Susan can cope with, and she doesn't work.'

Nicola was used to men asking this question. Usually it came with the unspoken accusation that she was just being greedy, which was a bit rich coming from a banker as it so often did. Because I *want* them and I can *afford* them, she felt like saying; because I'm thinking of the future, when I retire at fifty; because, *more life*; because – why *not*?

But this man was not attacking her, he was in his befuddled way genuinely curious.

'I would never have had so many if I'd had to stay at home and look after them myself,' she said, as she always said, to take the heat off. Then she continued, less guarded because she liked this man – 'I mean, I was tempted during my third pregnancy to take some time off. Charlie was seriously worried about the mortgage, I can tell you. I'd had a bad run of nannies. I'd missed all Jade's sports days

101

and prize-givings that year because of work. But as soon as the scan showed it was twins, that did it. I knew I'd be back at work as soon as I could crawl out of the house. Twins!'

'Susan says a nanny wouldn't be the same,' Iain persisted. He was pushing it now. 'She says they want *her* there.'

'Yes they'd prefer a mother at home,' said Nicola crisply. 'But I couldn't do that. I'm their mother, that's what they've got.'

Iain sat, shaking his head dolefully, and staring into his glass. Irritated, Nicola shifted in her seat and turned towards Donald.

'You'll be looking forward to the Reply from the Lassies,' he said.

'More?' said Nicola in horror, without thinking. He laughed.

'This should be the last. Truly.'

In the distance a young woman could be seen standing at the microphone consulting her notes.

'Isn't that Fiona MacPherson's new assistant?' asked Donald, leaning over her towards Iain. She felt his weight against her arm. 'Fiona MacPherson that's head of H.R. at the Auld Scotia?'

'Don't mess with that MacPherson woman, I'm telling you,' said Iain, mournfully shaking his head. Drink turned him into a clown, noticed Nicola.

'Behind every successful man there's a woman,' began the young woman at the microphone, and her voice was surprisingly loud and clear. 'Behind every successful woman is . . . what? That is the question I'd like to consider this Burns Night.'

Here we go, thought Nicola. What every woman needs

is a wife. She saw Donald raise an eyebrow at Brian Mahon, and Brian Mahon reply with a comical turning down of the corners of his mouth. Did this girl realise how little people liked to be lectured, wondered Nicola, wincing for her, and at the same time admiring her; more particularly how men hate to be lectured by women?

'Men ask, what is it women want?' the girl continued.

'A thundering scalade right enough!' shouted a frisky Scot on his eleventh whisky.

The most hurtful thing always was the assumption that because she was successful at work she must have sacrificed her children; that her children must have suffered. But if anybody had suffered, she now saw, it was her.

'Women want love and they want work, just the same as men,' declared the girl. 'And they want children to be seen as a fact of life not as a personal weakness. So if you love your women, all you men out there, take your share of what's called women's work so that us women can take some of the bread-winning burden off *your* shoulders. Get a life. Outside the office. It'll be better for your health. Better for your love life. And, if you're interested, since Burns mentions it, better for your immortal soul. *Aux armes, citoyens*! In the name of the love you claim to feel for us lassies.'

She left the dais to ragged applause and uncertain wolf whistles. She did not smile or look back.

'Well, for the majority of us, of course, that's luckily the case, the bit about having the wife at home taking care of all that side of things,' chuckled Iain Buchanan. 'And don't think it's not appreciated, Susan, because it is! Sorry, Nicola. But it's true. I can't see any reason why I should change a state of affairs that works, that allows me to work.

Let's face it, this sort of job needs total support and backup. We all need a bonny Jean to keep the home fires burning.'

'I suppose that was what you might call a professional suicide note,' said Donald. 'I wonder if Fiona MacPherson vetted that little diatribe. I rather think not.'

'And I'm not having some fat hen from H.R. telling me how to run my life. Or how to have weans, for Chrissake,' continued Iain. 'Pass that bottle of Deanston's, Brian.' He waved his quaich in the air. 'Freedom and whisky gang thegither.'

'I must say I've never heard that lesson drawn from Burns' life before,' mused Donald. 'Burns the family man. By all accounts he was the ultimate bastard when it came to loving them and leaving them.'

'He looked after his bairns, though,' said Iain hotly.

'Excuse me,' said Nicola. 'I was under the impression that it was his mother and his wife who looked after them. If I understood rightly.'

'Haw hey,' said Iain, fuddled. 'Right enough. But he didnae leave them to die in a ditch.'

'The trouble is, these days at work you have to put in the hours and be *sheen* to be putting in the hours,' said Brian Mahon, very slurred. 'I mean in a proper job. Not just teaching or journalism.'

'No, you couldn't call being a poet a proper job,' agreed Nicola, following her own line of thought. 'What did they used to say about Friday being Poet's Day? Piss Off Early Tomorrow's Saturday, that's right. Whereas Friday in this day and age is Dress Down day.'

'He did have a proper job, he was a farmer,' said Iain. 'He just didnae do very well at it. Then he was an exciseman. He was no idler.'

Hours are not a measure of love, Nicola assured her children; the number of hours 1 spend with you has nothing to do with how much I love you; you can ring me at work any time you want. Which was probably just what these three men, Iain and Donald and Brian, said to their wives. This man Donald had a lovely mouth, she noticed. She lifted her eyes and saw he was glowering at her.

'Family man,' he said, and his voice was hard and flat. 'That's the euphemism for a lazy bastard not pulling his weight.'

They lapsed into silence, broodingly, as more music started up. The piano was some way across on the other side of the hall, and Nicola could not see who was playing. If you got them up to Grade IV by the age of ten, you could enter them for a music scholarship. They hadn't twigged, first time round with Jade and Harry, but by the time the twins were born they'd got wise to it. Hence the Suzuki lessons.

Allowing herself at last to listen to the music, its solitary thoughtful quality affecting her like alcohol, she relaxed for the first time that evening. She let go, and of course that was a mistake.

Usually she bowed to the tyranny of postive thinking as anything clse was not exactly very helpful. Now fissures of doubt and ambivalence raced along the walls of the fortress. Charlie was off to Australia next week and she would be in Frankfurt. She wasn't easy when they were both out of the country at the same time. Harry had recently been diagnosed as dyspraxic, but she simply hadn't had time to follow it up. The nanny had been with them so long that she regarded herself as part of the family. And she wasn't. So *that* would end badly. Roderick

MacKenzie was buried and dead, a man of forty-three, and Charlie's PA had just been diagnosed as having breast cancer, and she was only thirty-eight. Burns had been thirty-seven, but that was then. She was older than that, they were all getting older all the time. As for sex, it was efficient these days but not exactly exciting. The pilot light was still there and the usual procedure led to a reliable enough firing up. But it had become something that was good for them, like going to the gym. Where was the wild restlessness she could hear in this music? She was aware of Donald Forfar's solid unfamiliar body beside hers, and wondered whether he was very hairy. She wouldn't mind. What a coward she was to have slept with only one man since marriage. You have one life, and the way to keep your life alive was through the sexual flame, she had seen that tonight, falling in love with new others, the tinder heart catching fire again and again. Yet *she* had chosen monogamy.

The piano playing drew to a close. Never had an evening gone on quite like this before. Those on her table had been bearing each other company for many hours like a little band of passengers in a lifeboat, and were now sagging with fatigue and alcohol. When yet another tartan-clad lassie walked up to the microphone clasping her hands soulfully before her, several of them clearly wished to lay their heads on the tablecloth in front of them and give up. Brian Mahon looked less than half-conscious. Charlie was rolling his eyes. This is ridiculous, thought Nicola; how are we supposed to get up in the morning after this? It's not like we've got the weekend to recover. It's a Wednesday. It's probably Thursday by now actually. She felt angry and sad. A bread roll flew through the air past the next table leaving a wake of tutting.

The girl's voice made a rich pompous warbling noise above them, but at least you could hear all the words.

> John Anderson my jo, John,
>   When we were first acquent;
> Your locks were like the raven,
>   Your bonny brow was brent;
> But now your brow is beld, John,
>   Your locks are like the snow.
> But blessings on your frosty pow
>   John Anderson my Jo.

'Jo means sweetheart,' whispered Donald. 'It's a song from an old wife to her wrinkled old baldy husband.'

She felt his whispering breath in her hair, and glowed. His arm was touching hers and it seemed to give off heat.

> John Anderson my jo, John,
>   We clamb the hill the gither;
> And mony a canty day, John,
>   We've had wi' ane anither:
> Now we maun totter down, John,
>   And hand in hand we'll go;
> And sleep the gither at the foot,
>   John Anderson my Jo.

'And are you looking forward to tottering down towards old age with your wife eventually?' she asked Donald politely, daringly, once it was finished.

He scowled at her as if through a cloud.

'My wife's just left me.'

'Oh, ah. *Ah*,' said Nicola. 'I'm sorry.'

Charlie's voice, slurred and fruity, drifted across the table.

'It's a braw licht moonlicht nicht the nicht. You see, I have a very *good* Scotch accent,' he was boasting to Susan Buchanan's glassy smile. He turned his head and gradually focused an eye on Nicola and her demon lover.

'Donald whar's yur troosers?' he demanded, dissolving into foolish sleepy laughter.

Then they were dazedly hauling themselves to their feet. The end had heaved into sight. Big Dougal was thanking them for coming and hoping they would all join in singing Burns' most famous song of all; but first he would like to thank . . .

Nicola turned to Iain Buchanan, who stared at her angrily.

'That poor bastert Burns,' he growled. 'Always on the edge of bankruptcy, the farm failing. All those mouths to feed, those women and children. Never any fucking security.'

'I suppose not,' said Nicola, thinking, I'm glad I'm not the one who's responsible for getting you home. All the way to Guildford, too.

'He worked hard to keep his family,' said Iain fiercely, as though she were denying it. 'When he didnae make it as a farmer he changed his career, he became an exciseman. Did you know that? He wasnae a drinker. The occasional bender like us all, *then* he might end up having one too many, but right enough he wasnae a drinker.'

'No, no,' said Nicola.

'It was the rheumatoid endocarditis, actually,' said Donald. 'That killed him.'

'Naw, he didnae die of drink, you know,' said Iain Buchanan, his face up close to hers, belligerent, and she realised he was very drunk. 'It wasnae the drink.'

'So you said,' said Nicola.

She could see Susan Buchanan staring across at her husband with a look of hopeless hungry grief.

'Burns was dying,' Donald Forfar announced in his stately fashion. 'The doctor sent him off alone to the Solway Firth. The doctor's orders were, to wade out to sea daily until he was up to his armpits, then to stand there in the freezing cold grey Atlantic for as long as he could. For some reason this did not improve his health. Then a bill for seven pounds and four shillings arrived from his tailor, and it struck deathly fear in his heart. He was hard pressed for money and he could not pay it. It became a gigantic sum in his mind, a horrifying debt. It tormented him. A few days later he was dead.'

Iain Buchanan gave a groan and tossed another few gills of whisky down his throat.

'That's very sad,' said Nicola, recognising for a fact that Iain had, in banking parlance, over-extended himself.

The pipers started up their wailing. It was nearly one o'clock. Side by side around the tables the guests stood up and swayed with varying degrees of self-consciousness and tiredness to the dismal strains of Auld Lang Syne.

> Should auld acquaintance be forgot
> And never brought to mind?
> Should auld acquaintance be forgot,
> And auld lang syne!

She wouldn't care if she never saw any of them again. Her right hand was in Iain's, who was on her left, and her left hand was in Donald's, who was on her right. She felt uneasy, as though she had become a conduit for their misery, which was, in each case, both inflammable and sodden, dangerously so, and not to be trusted.

'I'm in the middle of my life,' thought Nicola. 'I'm rooted in. I have four healthy children.' She felt a wave of gratitude break over her head.

Donald and Iain were gripping her hands too hard, Iain was droning away about cups o' kindness.

'I work hard, I earn good money, I'm able to take care of my family,' she added to herself. 'My precious children. *And* I'm not a drunk.'

Verse followed verse of Auld Lang Syne to general incomprehension, even among the Scots. Then it did end. It was over, and people were sheepishly seizing their neighbours for hugs and kisses, unable to meet each other's eyes. It was like the cringe-making conclusion to a happy clappy evangelical service, she thought; forced contact. Although the emotion here was more what you might call fearful tearful. Or just plain maudlin.

Donald Forfar grabbed her to him and kissed her on the mouth. Oh good, was her first thought, before common sense kicked in, and she closed her eyes and leaned into his hot body, into the heat and darkness of the kiss. She even liked the smell and the taste of the whisky. Again, like everything else that night, it seemed to last forever, though it couldn't have been more than a few seconds.

Then Charlie was beside them saying, 'Hey, excuse me,' very unsteady on his feet. He started to prod Donald on the shoulder when Iain stepped in and growled, 'Whit ye think ye're doing to ma friend?'

'Your friend?' said Charlie, looking baffled.

'Are you deaf, pal?' snarled Iain, 'Or just plain stupid?'

'Are you talking to me, Jocko?' said Charlie, turning away from Donald and squaring up to Iain.

'Een! Een!' squeaked Susan Buchanan, hopping around them and plucking at his sleeve. 'Come away from him! Come away now!'

Nicola went to join in, but found she was about to start laughing uncontrollably and so held back. It wasn't funny, it wasn't in the least bit funny. Donald touched her arm but she shrugged it off. No, I don't want you, she thought. I really don't. Rabbie Burns notwithstanding, that would be a very bad idea indeed.

Bystanders from the neighbouring tables stood gawping in a circle as though they could not believe their eyes. Iain got hold of Charlie's lapels and Charlie got hold of Iain's lapels. This wouldn't do her relationship with the Bank much good, realised Nicola, and her mind leaped ahead inventing damage limitation strategies. The men were both so stupefied with whisky that they could barely stand.

'*Naw*, Ee-yen,' screeched Susan Buchanan, 'Heh *naw!*'

Wrestling like two sleepy bears in a snowdrift, they fell, growling, slowly and heavily, the Scotsman and the auld enemy, down onto the white tablecloth at which they had sat politely facing each other for so many hours that night, crashing into the china and cutlery with a noise that was enough to bring a moment's silence to the rest of the vast room.

I even love my husband, thought Nicola in that moment, continuing to count her blessings. Even now. She watched him as he sprawled and brawled in the churning tartan-flashing stramash of bottles and leftovers. You are the father of my children, she said silently. But don't push it too far. Pal.

Opera

'But you love opera,' he said. 'Particularly the early stuff. I know you do.'

'Yes,' she said. 'I do.'

'So what's the problem?' he said. 'Try that red thing on now.'

She was standing in her underwear with clothes heaped round her feet, while he lolled on the bed. Since the children and then the loss of her job she had retreated into a shambles of soft leggings and sweatshirts, merely day versions of her pyjamas, except on occasions like now, when, kicking and screaming, she was dragged out for Client Entertainment. Then Christopher showed sudden interest in what she wore, as keen-eyed on the effect of this or that dress as any old-style libertine.

'Front stalls, gala performance,' he persisted. '*Orpheus and Eurydice*. Just right for a wedding anniversary, I'd have thought. Hold your stomach in, Janine. No, it's still no good. Try that black skirt again with the beaded top.'

'It's just about my favourite opera of all,' she panted, hating her reflection in the mirror. 'So fresh and unencumbered and straight to the heart. But.'

'But what,' he said.

'But not with clients,' Janine said reluctantly, as she knew this would enrage him.

'What difference does it make? They're all perfectly all right people. You're always on about how you like people.'

When he talked like this, she regarded it as a temporary madness in his life which she would have to put up with, like Pamina walking through the fire with Tamino, and have faith that they would be together again once he was over it.

'Clients aren't friends,' she said.

'They *can* be,' he said. 'You're so narrow-minded. They can become very *good* friends.'

'No,' she mumbled. 'Clients are about money.'

'Oh, wicked Mammon,' he hooted. '*Everything's* about money if you're talking in that ignorant way. Music certainly is. Look at Covent Garden for goodness' sake!'

'Clients are business,' she persisted, 'Not pleasure.'

'Client entertainment is *all about* pleasure,' he snarled. 'Good tickets, champagne, the works. You used to be more generous-spirited.'

'You can't get drunk with clients,' she said.

'You certainly can,' said Christopher. 'I do.'

'True,' she conceded. 'But you couldn't ever be really rude or insulting to clients.'

'You won't keep many friends that way either.'

'You don't make friends for their usefulness,' she said. 'There can't be strings attached.'

'Why not?' he said. 'Mutually beneficial relationships, that's the way the world works. *Special* relationships; hadn't you heard? Symbiotic's the word. Hadn't you *noticed?*'

'Is that why you married me?' she asked. 'Because of what I could do for you?'

'Obviously *not*,' he said with some truculence.

There was silence. He looked her straight in the eye.

'No,' he said.

'Good,' she said, and went and lay beside him on the bed.

'Your smell,' she said at last, her face in his shoulder. 'That's how I know it's still you.'

'Music! Me, I'm mad for it,' said Nigel Perkins from Littleboy and Pringle. 'All sorts. Depends on my mood. Verdi when I'm down. Which isn't often. A bit of Bowie. Some Cajun. Eine Kleine Nachtmusik. It's like food really, isn't it. Like Shakespeare said.'

Janine nodded and smiled.

'It's what you're feeling like at the time,' he continued. 'I usually listen in the car to be honest, or on the Walkman. Like most of us. So this'll be a novelty.'

'Do you know the story?' asked Janine.

'No,' he said. 'I guess I'll pick it up as I go along.'

'Um, but they're singing in French,' said Janine. 'It's the Berlioz version. Orpheus was a singer whose music charmed the wild beasts. Then his wife Eurydice died suddenly. He went down to the underworld looking for her . . .'

'Janice, Janice,' he said. 'It's OK! I get the drift.'

'Sorry,' said Janine.

'I think it ruins these things if you analyse them,' he said, looking round for more champagne. 'All that chatterchatterchatter.'

'Mmm,' went Janine.

'Ah, here's my wife. Penny! This is Christopher's wife, Janice.'

'Hi,' said Penny. 'Horrific journey, darling. Mega hold-up at Sevenoaks. Now, who's this Gluck fellow?'

'Born in Bohemia, studied in Italy,' said Janine before she could stop herself. 'Visited London, made friends with Handel, wrote an opera celebrating the Battle of Culloden, which flopped. Then he went to Vienna and . . .'

'Now then Janice!' said Nigel Perkins playfully. 'Chatter-chatterchatter.'

'The mummies on the bus go chatterchatterchatter,' sang Penny brightly.

'What?' said her husband.

'It's a nursery school song,' muttered Janine. 'Mine sing it too. The daddies on the bus go rustlerustlerustle. Their newspapers, you see.'

'Ladies and gentlemen, the performance is about to begin,' announced a waiter, shimmying up to their group and holding out a tray for empty glasses.

'Any idea how long it is to half time?' enquired Nigel Perkins.

'I'm not quite sure, sir, but I believe it's a very short opera.'

'That's good,' said Penny as they made their way to the auditorium. 'Time to enjoy the meal in the interval that way. Not like in *Pelléas and Mélisande*.'

'No, that was terrible!' agreed her husband. 'Massive long affair that was and only two fifteen-minute breaks.'

'Awful,' said Penny, shaking her head. 'Bolting down Coronation Chicken in the first interval, if you could *call* it an interval, then not very nice blueberry cheesecake in the second one and no time to finish your coffee. This is *much* nicer,' she said, turning to Janine with a gracious smile.

In the dark listening to the music Janine lifted away from the world of people and things. She forgot about the shadowy pinstripes each side of her and concentrated on the stage, where mourners like moving white statues tossed flowers on Eurydice's tomb. The bereaved husband Orpheus lay pole-axed by grief while the chorus of mourners sang their beautiful lament. 'Eurydice!' cried Orpheus, and she felt the frisson in her flesh. 'Eurydice!' he cried again, interrupting the mourners, and she sighed. Then for a third time he cried out 'Eurydice!' and this time she jumped, for Nigel Perkins was whispering in her left ear.

'That's cheerful,' he was hissing. 'Kicking off with a funeral.'

On stage the spirit of Hymen extinguished his torch to show marriage sundered by death, and the chorus sang:

> *L'amoureuse tourterelle*
> *Toujours tendre, toujours fidèle*
> *Ainsi soupire et meurt de douleur.*

Again Janine felt the unwelcome warmth of Nigel Perkins' breath in her ear.

'I said, *look*, they've got surtitles,' he whispered noisily. 'You needn't have worried about me after all.'

Janine forced herself to nod and smile.

'Nice of you, though,' he added, huskily.

At this point someone in the row behind shushed him and he settled back into his seat and shut up.

Was it marriage itself which had died, then, she wondered, returning to the other world; was it this ideal of turtle doves and fidelity, of the long-haul flight without betrayal, which had proved unworkable? Orpheus sang with mounting grief, urgent and controlled. It was coming back to her now, the particular quality of distress in this opera, where from the start something terrible has happened; something irreversible. And that's just like death, she thought. The line has been crossed and everything has changed.

The music had stolen up on her like hot water flooding over her skin. She remembered that morning in the half hour before waking, how a procession had trooped through her mind of all the people she had loved who were now dead. Last time Christopher had come home drunk from a client reception, she had wondered aloud whether he would notice if she died, and he had said how he bet she would *like* him dead then she would have no more pain or trouble. She stifled a groan.

Now Amour was informing Orpheus in cheery silvered tones that the Gods had taken pity on him and would allow him down into the infernal regions to fetch Eurydice back to life, on one condition. He must not look at her while in the precincts of the dead, nor tell her why not.

> *Soumis au silence*
> *Contrains ton desir*
> *Fais-toi violence*

sang Amour, and above the stage the surtitles slid past: In obedient silence Hold your longing in check Go against your every instinct. The words flew at her and landed in her like arrows. Wait in silence, yes, that was what was required of her, with the traditional carrot that love would be rewarded. But, she thought wrathfully, unlike in operas, we grow old while waiting in silence.

Orpheus was facing the Furies now, their rancorous music with booms and blaring from the horns, their flashing strings and fierce runs in octaves. He waited, then pleaded with the help of harp and flute to be allowed down to the kingdom of the dead. Again and again the Furies refused him, but at last his entreaties softened their hearts and they let him go. If only, thought Janine. When she said, I'm miserable, to Christopher, *he* said, No you're not. When she raged at him like one of the Furies, he said, I love you. Unfair. Unanswerable.

Back in the hospitality room at the interval, Christopher was all tenderness and attention, hovering dotingly over Dominic Pilling of Schnell-Darwittersbank and hanging on Dominic Pilling's wife's every word.

'London's getting terribly crowded, isn't it,' said the wife. 'Too many people. I'm afraid I'm a country girl at heart.'

'You love gardening,' Christopher suggested fondly.

'Oh yes. Except I get dreadful hayfever,' she said.

'So we have to get someone in to do it,' laughed Dominic.

'Because Dominic's not around enough at weekends to guarantee keeping it down,' she said.

'I have better things to do with my leisure time than cut the grass.'

'Like work,' she said nastily.

Janine caught Christopher's eye and looked away again. We'll be like them in five years' time, she thought, if we carry on like this; it's what you do every day that changes you.

'Ah leisure,' said Christopher hastily. 'That precious commodity. We're just in the process of booking ourselves a holiday, aren't we darling. Where did you go last time?'

'Club Med,' said Dominic Pilling with enthusiasm. 'Brilliant. The actual country you're in is irrelevant. They're all organised to the same very high standards so it hardly matters.'

'You don't have to lift a finger,' cooed his wife. 'The children are taken care of. You never see them! They adore it.'

'The main thing is to recharge the batteries,' declared Dominic.

'Are you enjoying the opera?' asked Janine.

'Oh it's super,' said his wife. 'And not too *long* either.'

Sitting in the dark again Janine realised that they had not been out on their own together that year. The music of Elysium came creeping in through her ears, slow, sublime, holding and catching her breath until she sighed deeply and shifted in her seat. He had no time for her. This must be what music was for, she thought, so while on the outside you moderated and rationalised and subdued, in your secret self you were allowed to live with an intensity not otherwise sanctioned. He was never there. Now the orchestral music became more complex, an oboe melody with rippling triplet accompaniment from the strings, braided like the surface of a fast-flowing river, or like the patterned weavings of thought and feeling, trouble and desire.

Eurydice was pleading with her husband to take her in

his arms. She sang her hurt in soft, slow, soaring phrases and descents. Why was he ignoring her? Was she no longer beautiful to him?

Janine felt a hot prickling sensation behind her face, like walking into a rosebush. Almost the worst thing was being frozen into these corny, passive and wifely attitudes of grief and betrayal. The ravishingly sweet quarrel of their voices blended and untangled, pulling air down into her lungs, making her sigh helplessly.

Eurydice sang, Dear husband, I can hardly breathe for sorrow. Orpheus was protesting his devotion and at the same time crushing her with his indifference. Then at last he cracked. He turned to look back at her. She died instantly. It was the least bombastic of operatic deaths, and the most comfortless. He had misjudged and this time she was lost forever.

As he began his famous aria, *J'ai perdu mon Eurydice*, Janine realised that tears were streaming down her face. For pity's sake, she thought, not here, and tried to wipe them away unobtrusively with the back of her hand. But they kept on coming. The next thing was that Nigel Perkins was smuggling his handkerchief into her lap and whispering something in her ear. What was he saying? It sounded like, One too many. That made her want to giggle, or spit at him. Luckily Christopher was at the other end of the row. She took some deep slow breaths and pushed the music away from her.

At least this was not an opera where the best was kept till last. The final two scenes were as unconvincing as ever, trundling on towards their unearned happy ending. As far as Janine was concerned, it was over already. She listened unmoved as Amour stopped Orpheus from killing himself and told him everything would be all right. She couldn't have cared less when he produced Eurydice like a rabbit from a hat before ascending to heaven on a cloud attended by zephyrs and cupids. By the time the last note had sounded, she was ready to go. First, though, there was the crashing tide of applause to wade through.

'Thank you for lending me your handkerchief,' she said to Nigel Perkins as they clapped on steadily, side by side. 'I sometimes get a bit swept away when I go to the opera.'

'My wife can't handle champagne either,' he said. 'I won't let her touch it.'

'Ah,' said Janine.

'It was a bit of a cop-out, the ending, I thought,' said Nigel, jerking his head towards the stage.

'Difficult to do the original, though,' she replied. 'Drunken maenads tear Orpheus into pieces and rip his head off.'

'There you are, you see,' grinned Nigel. 'Women and alcohol. Fatal combination. Keep the hanky by the way.'

'No thanks,' said Janine, handing it back. 'You cloth-eared berk.'

He stared at her as though he couldn't believe his ears; and, after all, she had spoken softly enough in the middle of all this noise for doubt to exist.

'But it was *sweet* of you to think of me,' she gushed, smiling at him gratefully and leaning across the arm of the seat to give him a peck on the cheek.

At last it was over, the queuing for coats, the milling around outside in the night air and the hulloo'd thanks and farewells as cab doors slammed shut. When the last client had been tucked into a taxi and sent purring off into the darkness, Janine yawned a great yawn and finished this yawn with a growl. Christopher had switched off his hospitality smile and was giving her a wary look.

'Are you all right?' he said.

'Yup.'

'Goodgood.' He paused. 'The cabs seem to have dried up all of a sudden. You wait here, I'll go and find one.'

'I'm coming with you,' she said, but he was off.

She went wild. She started to run after him, but he was faster than her.

'Christopher,' she shouted.

He pretended not to hear.

'Christopher!' she yelled again.

He was a dark figure about to melt into the blackness.

'Christopher!' she bellowed with all her might and lung power.

He slowed down gradually, unwillingly, then stopped and stood where he was for a few long seconds before turning to look back at her.

Cheers

The frost which beautified the car that morning had turned it into something else, a hardened glacé fruit, the green of its paintwork obscured by a nap of crystal bristles. Inside, Lois tried the ignition a few more times and tutted at the engine's croupy yelping.

When she looked up at passing cars, she saw dazzled faces screwed into eyeless masks. The forecast had promised a windchill factor of minus twelve in the week to come. She couldn't get it to start so she would have to walk to the station.

All across Cator Park trees stood cold and fabulous, elaborately naked in their diamonds. Crack troops flashing silver from the windows of nearby houses charged into their leafless branches and ended up in smithereens. Lois stalked along the paths like a film star, collar up and hands thrust deep in pockets.

On the station platform she stood beneath a sweet and heartless blue sky with no warmth or depth to it. It would be much easier to live if it were always like this, thought Lois: thin-blooded, energetic, unsmudged. The other sort of December day – defeated outlook, wet pavements, fine mean sleet – was harder to take.

Once on the London Bridge train she opened that morning's Christmas cards, a batch of wassail cups and donkeys and gaitered snowballers, and studied the handwritten messages inside. So Jill had got her divorce after all. And here was Sally announcing that she and Gavin and their brood were moving to the country. On the whole Lois thought this a mistake which would lead to an increase in their morosity and paranoia. They were trying to twitch their coat hems away from the rest of humanity, and would spend their whole time in the car listening to story tapes. The main thing, thought Lois, looking out of the window at south London's back gardens, the important thing as middle age came and sat down on you with its enormous bum, the vital thing surely was, not to grow too careful of yourself.

She reviewed her arrangements for the rest of that day. The boys were at her childminder's and would stay overnight as she, Lois, was meeting an old college friend for a meal after the shops closed, and would be late back. And William could no longer be asked to do anything domestic like collect the children. His home was now less his castle than his garage.

In the last year he had been coming home later and later until it hardly seemed worth it, with eyes like fried eggs, completely unreachable, falling half-clothed dead asleep beside her. He wouldn't say what it was, if it was anything worse than not being young any more. He wouldn't talk to her. Last night she had seen by the landing light how he lay with his mouth half-open, a little pocket of rotten-fruit breath playing at its entrance, and she had been tempted to light a match a couple of inches above his teeth and watch the ghostly blue flames dance over his features.

At London Bridge she went underground, resurfacing at Oxford Circus on a wave of close-packed shoppers. Jammed together like this, sharing each other's warm and stale breath, shoulder against back or arm or ribcage, each struggled to preserve some inner distance by refusing to meet other eyes. I like being among people and not knowing them, even *this*, thought Lois; I like being part of the crowd. She surged across Oxford Street on another wave, then expertly up the escalators at John Lewis until she stood at a shelf of bolts of plastic-coated fabric. Cosiness was the worst of the Christmas cons, she decided as she rejected the Dingly Dell design.

Two metres should do it, she thought, examining the other patterns, envisaging her dining table with the extra leaf in it at two o'clock on Christmas Day. There was William at the head, well into the next bottle, blearily inaccessible. Beside him sat his mother, chatting her way round the orbital loop of early Alzheimer's. Then there were her boys, rolling sprouts at each other and at their cousins; and her younger sister, widowed that year, still electric with grief and terror; her elder sister, not even trying to look as though she were not hungering after her unfortunately married man at the head of his own groaning festive board; and their angry mother, sixty-eight, mouth stained with red wine, like a pike in claret.

'Two and a half metres please,' she said, as the man unwound a panorama of wipe-clean poinsettias. There they had all been, ready at the gates when she had woken early that morning, waiting to walk right into her mind and sit down and let her look after them. Beneath her duvet she had felt herself unravelled by rancorous pity, dismembered by tenderness and resentment.

The rest of the afternoon went in packed shops and glitter and cash. She had seen it all before, she knew just where to go and what to buy, but it still delighted her, choosing presents, because she was good at it. She was looking forward to seeing Holly too. She loved being out, talking about something outside herself. They were meeting in a Polish café Holly had chosen.

This café, Lois found, as she later consulted her map of the underground, was four stops down the Bakerloo line then five along District and Circle. Once on the train she sat discrete and silent beneath her carrier bags. Christmas had become one big advertising campaign for the family, but nobody pointed out how the family would close you down to the outside world given half a chance. She glanced appreciatively at the strangers around her, all ages and shapes and sizes.

There were faces foolish from office parties, and late guarded shoppers like herself. Beside her a tall black man sat reading an evangelical newsletter, while members of the Japanese group opposite were examining a programme for *The Phantom of the Opera*.

At the head of the carriage swayed a frisky, grizzled growler and crooner. He was conducting his own party, growing livelier by the minute. Now he was creeping up to women sitting alone, a Rumpelstiltskin on pointed toes of stealth, thrusting out his chin and snorting a whisky-drenched blast into their faces, laughing with delight when they jumped. He did it to Lois and in spite of herself she jumped like the rest. Next he skipped over to the Japanese group and stood there in front of it making slitty eyes and hooting with pleasure.

Lois smelt the whisky which fuelled him, and considered

the old theory of spontaneous combustion. His every organ must be saturated with Scotch, his veins running amber, his bodily tissues highly inflammable. The world was awash on a sea of alcohol, she realised, Russia, Scotland, Romania, the entire Eastern bloc. Oh, and Scandinavia too of course, its length and breadth, and don't forget the Low Countries.

Tired of teasing, he lurched across the carriage to a support rail against which he steadied himself, then took out a cigarette. Lois held her breath as he lit it with a clumsily struck match.

'There is no smoking on the underground trains,' came a voice sumptuous in its gravity.

It was the man beside her who had spoken.

Lois nearly jumped out of her skin. The rest of the carriage leant forward agog. The drunk narrowed his eyes incredulously at his challenger, then opened them clownishly wide, then narrowed them again.

'You must put out your cigarette,' said her neighbour.

When the drunk took a defiant drag and puffed smoke at him like a naughty boy, he rose from his seat, plucked out the cigarette between finger and thumb, and ground it underfoot. Then he sat down and resumed reading his Christian news.

Lois caught a cunning look on the drinker's face. She watched his hand creep towards the inside pocket of his mac in elaborate slow motion; as if, she thought, for a knife.

She got up and moved away and murmured about the knife to the young Australian she found herself standing beside. No worries, he said, there's no knife, and anyway he's a big guy, he can take care of himself. But sheer bone and heft are no protection against steel, she thought, uneasy as the train at last drew in to Piccadilly Circus. The drinker darted up to his reprover and shook his hand as though they were old friends, unleashing as he did so some incomprehensible truism about life, or death; then nipped off the train at the last minute with a merry farewell wave of his hand.

Every woman who left the train after that made a point of sidling past the hero on her way out and muttering some praise or thanks. He acknowledged each tribute with a nod, and continued to read. Lois, who had gone back to her seat, turned to him and murmured that it had been brave of him but shouldn't he be careful in case of a knife? He turned and looked at her with unsmiling eyes.

'Someone has to stand up and say it,' he said.

'I suppose so . . .' she began.

'There is too much freedom,' he told her, closing down the conversation.

Too much freedom, she thought, as she changed trains at Embankment. Too much freedom! That's not the sort of moral you want to hear. Not from a hero.

Holly was already at a corner table sipping from a litre of Bulgarian red when Lois appeared with her shopping.

'There was a drunk on the train,' began Lois, struggling out of her coat.

'All those ossif parties,' said Holly. 'I hate it when they vomit and you still have several stops to go. Let me pour you a glass.'

'Cheers,' said Lois. 'Are your sixth formers all coming in with hangovers?'

'Fourth years up,' said Holly. 'I think we should give

them compulsory lines in December. Write out a hundred times, I must drink a pint of milk before I go down the pub.'

'Or they could choose instead, Never drink when you're angry, lonely, tired, hungry or bored.'

'So, never,' said Holly. 'Basically. Cheers.'

'They'll all be at raves soon,' said Lois, raising her glass. 'Safe from the Demon Drink.'

'Red wine is *good* for you,' said Holly as she glugged away, 'Although it has to be at least four units a day before there's any effect on the bad-cholesterol lipoproteins.'

'I needed that,' said Lois. 'This sentimental line on the family they trot out every Christmas, it makes me angry; as though there's some transformative magic wood.'

'I blame Dickens,' said Holly. 'The memory of sorrow softens the heart. Does it hell.'

'Such cosiness,' Lois hissed, glaring at the menu. 'Such lies. I can't think of a single family that *isn't* dysfunctional in some way. That's what they're *for*.'

They studied the list, its *barszcz*, its stuffed cabbage in white sauce and its meatballs in red.

'I'm ravenous,' said Holly. 'Meatballs for me. I've come straight from a very long nativity play. Dave's youngest was a shepherd.'

'The boys had theirs yesterday,' said Lois. 'You know the bit when there's no room at the inn? They said, "Unfortunately everywhere is fully booked".'

'How very Sydenham,' said Holly. 'We don't get that sort of language out in Ilford.'

They ate and drank and discussed Holly's plans to abandon teaching and go into computer programming. Although she thought this might drive her mad with boredom it would pay enough to enable her and her partner Dave to move out of her flat and into a house; and since Dave's children were staying most weekends now this had its advantages. His wife still would not give him a divorce. His children blamed her, Holly, for their parents' separation. She and Dave wanted their own baby but she had had a miscarriage last year and time was running out. Meanwhile her own father's second wife had left him a couple of weeks ago and he too would be coming to Holly's for Christmas.

Lois listened to more about Dave's vile wife, his malevolent children, about how it was Dave's duty to himself they were ignoring, and noticed how this always happened with Holly now after the first few drinks. She lost her honesty. She would look at the complicated and painful equation she and Dave had had to draw up in order to be together, then she would have another drink and boldly claim the moral high ground as well. This was all done in what Lois privately called Polonius-speak.

'What do *you* think?' asked Holly at last, staring at her with a certain loss of focus.

'I'm on the side of love and happiness,' said Lois tactfully.

'So how's William these days?' asked Holly, ordering another half-litre of wine without reference to Lois.

'I don't really know,' said Lois. 'He's stopped talking to me and he's drinking too much.'

'Make him say limericks,' said Holly with relish, then attempted the one about round the rugged rock but fell at the third syllable.

Lois watched her heaving with giggles and realised almost casually that William had borrowed more money from somewhere, without telling her, and had lost it again. That was why he could not talk to her. Her thoughts strode ahead of her in seven-league boots.

By the end of the meal Holly had drunk a good deal. Her eyes looked skewwhiff, as though they were trying to regroup on the same side of her nose, like a flounder. She was challenging Lois' memory as to the origins of English carols, which had been the subject of a college essay they had both tackled twenty years ago. It was hot chocolate then, thought Lois.

'Lullay, lullay,' sang Holly, causing heads to turn, 'Thou little tiny child . . .' and her voice cracked and her face weakly crumbled.

'It's that tune,' she whispered as Lois hastily paid the bill and passed her tissues under the table.

Oh hell, thought Lois, Oh bloody hell, while trying to hail a taxi and reassure her that nobody had noticed.

'I'll be all right,' mumbled red-eyed Holly, tripping over a carrier bag. 'Got a return ticket.'

'Ilford please,' said Lois, giving her a cross hug and bundling her into the back of a black cab, countering the driver's obvious lack of enthusiasm for his fare with a twenty-pound note up front.

'She all right then?' said the driver, casting a leery look over his shoulder at the figure slumped across the back seat.

'Of course she's all right,' snapped Lois, slamming the door. 'She's a teacher.'

The trains were in chaos that night but she took one as far as Lewisham, then caught a bus which was destined eventually to pass through Lower Sydenham. She even had a seat on the end of the three-person banquette behind the driver, with a large sleepy woman lolling between her and the man at the other end.

'Stay awake,' said the man now and then into the sleepy woman's ear. When he stood up to get off the bus at the corner of Catford Road, the woman tottered after him and crashed to the pavement. That seemed to rouse her a little, and she looked up into the bus with a puzzled expression and said, 'Drummond Road?'

'She's not with me,' called the man to the driver. 'Says her stop's Drummond Road.'

'Anybody getting off at Drummond Road might see this lady right?' called the driver down the bus into the crowd of blank embarrassed faces.

Oh *bloody* hell, thought Lois.

'I am,' she said grimly, helping haul the woman back on. Her black tights had split into a web of white holes and wet red knees.

'Shorry darling,' the woman slurred, and slumped against her on the seat and fell asleep.

'Wake *up*,' said Lois. 'What's your name?'

'Treesa,' mumbled the woman. '*Tess*. Tess.'

'Come on Tess. It's our stop next. Drummond Road.'

'Drummond Road,' said Tess sitting up, eyes closed.

'You be all right then?' said the bus driver as Lois, festooned with carrier bags, helped her down.

'*I* don't know, do I,' snapped Lois, followed through the window by thirty pairs of eyes as the bus drove off.

'Drummond Road,' she said loudly. 'What NUMBER? Stay awake!'

'Hundred shirty sor. Shirty sick,' said Tess, fishing out

an enormous bunch of keys and handing them over. Her eyes were closing again.

'A hundred and thirty-*four*?' shouted Lois. 'Thirty-*six*?'

'Kiss,' said Tess with a great effort. 'Shirty kiss. Hunnard shirty kiss.'

'A hundred and thirty-SIX?'

'Us,' said Tess exhaustedly. She was wearing stilettos, which made her lurch fearsomely, but she would not take them off.

'Keep going,' said Lois through gritted teeth. It was like coaxing along a gigantic toddler.

At number 136 she tried every key on the bunch without success. She pressed the seven doorbells in turn, but nobody answered. She tried the keys again. On the second time round the lock gave and they were in. Tess led the way up the carpetless stairs and as Lois followed her she glimpsed one of the downstairs lodgers open his door a crack. She saw a slice of a face, the glitter of an eye, and then the crack closed noiselessly.

'Smine,' said Tess exhaustedly, indicating a door on the landing. Then she went into the lavatory beside it and bolted herself in.

'Oh bloody hell,' said Lois, putting down her carrier bags and going through the business with the keys again, twice, because this door had two separate locks. It opened at last.

'Are you all right in there?' she called to Tess through the bolted door.

'I'm grand, darling,' came Tess's voice, with effortful enunciation. 'Don't you worry about me then.'

'But you'll come out in a minute?' called Lois.

'Sure I will, baby.'

Lois picked up her bags and pushed her way into the room. There was a brown-sheeted bed with clothes heaped all over it and round it on the floor. The kitchen sink in the corner held underwear soaking in a plastic washing-up bowl, a wooden spoon sticking out as though to stir it. There was nothing else except two Christmas cards above the blocked-in fireplace, and a huge bare fir tree which almost touched the ceiling.

Lois rinsed the cups and mugs on the draining board, filled them with cold water and set them up by the bed. She held her breath and emptied the underwear into the sink, then put the bowl down by the bed too. Next she pleaded and bullied through the bolted door for the woman to come out.

'All right darling,' came the reply in conciliatory tones. 'All right. I'll get you something to eat, baby. Can I get you something to eat?'

'But first of all you must come out,' begged Lois. 'Please.'

The woman said she loved her, and offered to feed her again. Lois leant against the wall and closed her eyes.

'*Please* come out,' she repeated. She was nearly finished. She had had enough.

The door rattled open at last, with Tess emerging like a big shamed child, clutching more underwear.

'It's all right,' clucked Lois, faint with relief. 'Don't worry. It doesn't matter.'

'I'm shorry, darling,' moaned Tess. 'I'm *shorry* shorry.'

The vulnerability of this big soft woman, her gaping handbag, her bunch of keys so readily handed over and really the lack of fight in her, made Lois think back almost with nostalgia to the spiteful goblin on the train. She helped Tess onto the bed, where she curled in a foetal hump and, growling, pulled the covers tightly over her head.

Lois stepped back to the door and realised she was holding her breath. The main thing now was to leave Tess *inside* the room, with her handbag and keys beside her; and for her, Lois, to be *outside* the room, with her carrier bags, pulling the door shut. This she managed. Her heart was thumping hard with tiredness and uselessness and she clumped down the hollow stairs as fast as she could, with a panicky apprehension on her way out that she would have to pass a wolf at the door on his way up.

Outside in the cold she felt safe again. She walked on for a while past kebab bars and minicab offices, then noticed a rip-roaring bevy of boys at the next pub, and decided to turn off the main road. The side streets would be a quieter route home, even if they took longer. In their tiny front gardens ivy leaves had been chilled to shagreen, and all the leaves on the privet hedges were pewter-plated. That's what I want, she thought; I want to be pewter-plated.

The curtains in this road had mostly been left undrawn, and at nearly every window glowed a well-lit tree in a darkened room. When she got home she would open the front door and there would be the tree she and the boys had decorated two days ago. She was very tired. She trudged on under the street lamps. Safe as houses. Safe as trees. Sane as trees. Mad as trees. Why had Tess dragged that mad great tree up into her room? What business had a tree inside a house anyway? You shouldn't let trees indoors, they belonged outside.

The house would go too, that was it. And he couldn't tell her. Bloody *hell*, she thought, stopping in her tracks. Why couldn't he tell me that before, she wondered. I know why, he thinks it's a competition and he's failed. So that's what it is, she thought, relieved after all the silence; though of course it was terrible. Better out than in, though. So to speak. She stood heaving gale-force sighs and shaking her head.

A church clock struck the hour, lengthily. It was midnight. She heard the chugging past of a distant night bus, and laughter from people leaving a house further along the road. When she looked up at the roofs of the houses she saw there was a white velvet pelt of frost on the tiles, just as there was on the slats of the garden fences. This frost glittered superbly in the glow from the street lamps.

A forest of trees stood shining in their front-room havens, winking their fairy lights at her as she stood out on the pavement. Round the rugged rock the ragged rascal ran. The rooms which sheltered them would be balmy with spice, evergreen and zest. In the light of their beauty she felt a kick of stubborn happiness as well as everything else. She blew her nose like a trumpet. Then she picked up her carrier bags of presents one by one, and set off on the rest of the walk home.

Wurstigkeit

'What have you told them at work?' she asked. 'What have you told them at yours?' I countered.

'I don't need to tell them anything,' she said, looking down her long nose at me unsmilingly. 'I'm in charge.'

We had met as arranged on the pavement outside the Huguenot house in Fournier Street, the one whose area railings are headed with thistles rather than spears. I had been out east that morning to see the man at the Regulators about some recent embarrassing losses suffered by Leviathan Bank, whose compliance department I was running. On the way back from Canary Wharf to my lunchtime assignation in Spitalfields I had had the bad luck to be driven by one of those furious obsessive cabbies who hate traffic and know a thousand secrets about London's backstreets. He scorned the obvious routes, refused Commercial Road, shot off up in the direction of Bow then lost his temper at the first red light and tore off round Salmon Lane to grind to a swearing, cursing and of course entirely foreseeable halt on the Mile End Road. I was feeling mildly sick by this point but he would not be satisfied until he'd swung us madly north up into Bethnal Green. At Weavers

Fields I began to despair of ever escaping, but then at last he dropped me at the top of Brick Lane, expressing indignant incredulity at the one-way system, which, as any child knows, is nothing if not long-established.

Even so, I was early. I was feeling buoyant and restless when I looked forward to the next hour or so. While I waited for Isobel Marley, I watched an old man running for a bus which had overshot the stop. He was creeping along, legs low down like a jaguar stealthily approaching its prey through the rainforest, with a broad ingratiating grin of pain on his face. I'm not really young any more, it came to me, wincing in sympathy; but then (cheering up) I'm not that old yet either.

Isobel's black cab drew up at last, gleaming and purring. She took her time unpacking her long-limbed full-bellied self from the back. It had taken her over twenty minutes just from Gray's Inn Road, and she made the driver write out a receipt. We exchanged nods, avoiding each other's eyes. Guilt and complicity hovered in the air like creaky old stage conventions.

'So,' she said, after we had exchanged formal greetings. 'Where is this secret cavern of temptation?'

'I'm not allowed to say,' I said, truthfully. 'You'll just have to follow me.'

'That's ridiculous!' she hissed as I led her down past Fashion Street and the police station, then left into Chicksand Street. 'Ludicrous! Who do they think they are?'

I had met Isobel Marley two days before at Iddon Featherstone's reception for their corporate finance clients in Seething Lane. Iddon Featherstone is a smallish law firm and its partners are always hoping I'll put work their way.

Sometimes I do. I went along this time because I'm curious about their mooted merger with the German law firm Marbeiter Rotenhart, which is looking both inevitable and, for some Iddon Featherstone partners, disastrous.

'The trouble is, Laura, we need more than a toehold in Frankfurt,' fretted John Mannion, head of Corporate Finance. 'We may not like it but we've got to bite the bullet.'

'Difficult,' I commiserated, taking a sip of mineral water. I glanced round the room. It was a picture by Manet rather than Monet. Everyone there was in the self-concealing monochrome of corporate life. The only flashes of colour to contradict the moonlit effect were provided by the men's ties.

Not far from us a very tall strong-featured woman stood talking to Iddon Featherstone's managing partner, Graham Groton. She must have been six or seven months pregnant, and I couldn't help thinking how much better pregnancy looks in tailored worsted than in the more traditional maternity smocks.

'Of course, it's the way the whole world's having to go now,' I said. 'There's been a positive stampede of mergers in the broking sector. Everyone's very jumpy.'

We both watched as a waiter approached and the tall woman held out her glass for more champagne.

'That's illegal now, isn't it?' said John Mannion. 'Boozing while up the duff? You'd get lynched in the States for less than that.'

'Good luck to her,' I said.

'It'll be her fourth,' said John Mannion, and for a moment I thought he was referring to her alcohol intake.

'Isobel Marley QC. She's done a great job for us on that money laundering case in the Philippines.'

'Oh yes,' I frowned, recognising the name from an article about high-flying women in that week's *Financial Times*. 'In the Updraught.'

We watched Graham Groton raise his glass to her. He is rather short, Graham, and she was having to talk down to him.

'I only like tall men,' I said flippantly.

I'd been working like a maniac towards the CGGI deal that the board kept insisting should go ahead despite all the counter indications of shadiness I had been urging them to consider. My integrity was on the line. The man I had met earlier that year and whom I might, given time, have grown to love, had understandably grown tired during this CGGI case of waiting until ten or eleven at night for my work-weary self to grace him with an hour or two, and had gone.

'I like to look up at a man,' I explained.

'To,' said John Mannion, with a startled roll of the eye. I realised he was several inches taller than me.

'No, at,' I said, and smiled.

'Ah,' he said. 'Got you. But let me introduce you to Isobel. You must meet her.'

Isobel Marley had been listening for long enough to Graham Groton's gung-ho line on the merger and how we were all now part of one big European family for her face to register as we approached a flash almost of joy. Only almost, for her face was singularly serious, impressively so, and, except for the odd luxury of a frown, impassive.

'But how *can* Europe be one big happy family,' I launched in, unable to let this go; it was Europe's various madly conflicting regulatory regimes which had kept me on fifteen-hour days these last two months. A deal which was whiter than white in one country could be distinctly off-colour in another and downright criminal in a third. The Euro wasn't the half of it.

'You must feel like the Lone Ranger,' chuckled John Mannion. 'You and the other compliance guys. Galloping around after the outlaws. Them thar traders.'

'Hi ho Silver,' I said. 'Someone's got to do it.'

'Not exactly bad news for law firms,' said Isobel, but her heart wasn't in it. She had been distracted; she had noticed what no man would ever notice.

At this point, John Mannion and Graham Groton were drawn away by another Iddon Featherstone partner to meet the *grauen emminenz* from Marbeiter Rotenhart, who was over in London on a rare dynastic visit.

Isobel paused, then allowed herself to comment, 'That's a nice shirt.'

I was wearing a white shirt with my grey suit, boringly meek and plain. Only a member of the unofficial ocular freemasonry would have noticed that it was made of nun's veiling, with a faint grey stripe the width of a pencil lead.

'Why,' I remembered asking the sales assistant at Wurstigkeit that time, staring hard at the beautiful but after all plain shirt, 'Why, um, is it *so* much money, this one?'

'Ah, this one,' he had replied. 'Look, there, the stripe, you see? It is because the line is broken.'

Sure enough there were minute sugar-grain sized gaps in the fine stripe.

'Of course,' I'd said. And bought it.

'Thank you,' I now said to Isobel.

I saw her struggling with herself. She was an intensely

142

competitive type, that much was obvious, and she would not be able to bear not to ask.

'It's nice cloth,' I taunted, almost laughing. 'Like down against the skin. And see, the line is broken.' I held out my cuff for inspection.

'So it is,' she said. 'Yes.'

She paused again, poker-faced, then could not help herself and asked, 'It's not from that shop, is it? That mad shop with the password where they won't give out their address? What's it called?'

'Wurstigkeit,' I said, blushing slightly.

'What a ludicrous idea, a shop with a password,' she scoffed.

She couldn't bear to feel excluded, it was obvious. She was used to being on every list, right at the top.

'It's eccentric,' I agreed, blithely.

'Isn't it terribly expensive?' she sniffed.

'Not to someone in the updraught,' I said. 'Surely.'

It was far too expensive for me now, but I wasn't going to tell *her* that. Since I first visited, Wurstigkeit's prices had quintupled, sextupled, rising by at least a hundred per cent each year. Market forces!

Five years ago I had met a man from Shibui Investments for lunch in a restaurant near Liverpool Street. He had been summoned by his mobile to an emergency deal-breaker before we had finished the *amuse-gueules* and so, finding myself with a rare uncharted hour, I had allowed myself to drift outside mapless into the dusty sun. It was at a point in my life when I could not sleep for worrying. I was starting to experience low-level panic attacks at night when I could hear my jumpy heart and ragged breathing as myriad horrors, regrets, fears and raw-heads hurtled towards me (lying doggo beside my now ex-husband pretending to sleep) in a shower of meteorites. I had taken to carrying with me in my briefcase a collection of small bottles of flowerdew remedies, each claiming to protect against a specific misery. The ones I used most were Rock Water, labelled 'For the self-repressed who overwork and deny themselves any relaxation,' and Wood Betony 'For those who find it difficult to love themselves.'

Anyway, it was during this window-like hour at a less than euphoric stage in my life that, by chance, I stumbled into Wurstigkeit, which had opened only that week. It was like stepping into the fabled wardrobe and finding yourself in another country. The point was, it was an experience in weightlessness. It subtracted your centre of gravity.

'Wurstigkeit,' said Isobel. 'I wonder what that means. Sausage something, it sounds like.'

'Laura,' said John Mannion, waltzing up with an older man in tow. 'Laura, I'd like you to meet Günter Mangelkammer. Herr Mangelkammer is head of Commercial Litigation over in Frankfurt. Herr Mangelkammer, this is Laura Collinson, head of Compliance at Leviathan. And this, this is the distinguished QC, Isobel Marley.'

'How fortunate,' said Isobel, smiling at Herr Mangelkammer. 'We were just puzzling over the meaning of a German word. Perhaps you will be able to help us.'

'I might be delighted,' said Herr Mangelkammer warily.

'What was it, Laura?' Isobel asked.

'Wurstigkeit,' I said.

'Ah yes,' said Herr Mangelkammer, visibly relieved. 'I know this. It is an expression introduced by Bismarck. It describes a mental state. How must I say? To do with sausages.'

'Sausages?' said John Mannion, his eyebrows in his hair.

'A state of sausage-like behaviour,' persisted Herr Mangelkammer.

'Sausageness,' I put forward.

'Sausageness is good,' he agreed. 'Meaning, people don't care. They don't care a sausage's worth.'

'They don't give a fig?' I offered.

'They don't give a fuck!' cried John Mannion, laughing heartily. 'They don't give a flying fuck!'

'Your way is better, I think,' said Herr Mangelkammer, honouring me with a nod.

We turned from Chicksand Street into Frostric Walk, then down a villainous urinous alley so narrow that where a moment before there had been enough blue sky above to cut out a pair of sailor's trousers, now there was nothing but a forget-me-not ribbon.

'Are you *quite* sure you know where we're going?' asked Isobel with some asperity as she picked her well-shod way between various noisome puddles.

We took a twist at the end here, then on to one last dark paved lane, and we had arrived.

'You must be joking,' said Isobel flatly, staring at the scuffed and numberless portal with the blacked-out picture window beside it.

She glanced at her watch with irritation, then at me.

'Wait a moment,' I said.

On the wall at the level where a doorbell should have been was the bas-relief head of a satyr, and into the ancient whorled ear of this creature I whispered the password. Then I stepped back and waited.

The door opened slowly on backward hinges, and we

followed. Inside, it was the hall of the Mountain King filled with the trousseau of his robber bride. I caught my breath, and started to feel bouncy and oxygenated, airy and greedy. My eyes lusted around all over the place. The colours teased and tingled and clashed like music, while the walls receded into velvety darkness. I tried to keep some semblance of indifference but the smiles kept crossing my lips, and soon I was cooing and clucking and gasping as I moved from rail to rail. Isobel riffled through this rack and that, pursing her lips. I saw the stuff through her eyes, as when I'd looked in for the first time five years ago. What a load of tat, I'd thought. What a heap of magpie rubbish, little bright bits of rubbish.

Then I'd suddenly got caught. Was it a corsair's slanted stripes down the front of a structured cardigan? I'd thought, how *can* they charge more than a fiver for this nonsense; and, a second later, the scales had fallen from my eyes. I'd understood that here was something indefensible at work, and had reached for my chequebook. It was the story of the Emperor's new clothes, but backwards.

Now Isobel was reaching for the price tags and huffing and puffing and casting stuff aside with a curled lip.

'Don't look at the price tags,' I advised. 'Look at the clothes.'

I took a long viridian garment from its hanger and held it out behind her. Instinctively she slid her arms back into the sleeves and shrugged it on. We looked at her guarded face in the long mirror, and at the grande dame opera coat whose plaited, puffy, serpentine collar she had drawn superbly up to her chin.

'No,' she said, casting it aside. 'I'd never wear it. *When* would I wear it?'

146

'That's not the point,' I started to say, but decided to wait.

Perhaps after all she was merely status-seeking, an acquisitive label-conscious shopper. If so, I had misjudged, and this was a waste of time.

I remembered that *FT* interview with Isobel Marley. A blur of phrases came back at me, things like, a hundred and twenty per cent, superleague, total commitment, that sort of stuff. She had been quoted as saying, 'I'm a workaholic, I'm fantastically good at what I do,' and had rejected the soubriquet of fatcat with talk of freedom and markets. That was all distinctly unpromising. Surely she had no *time* for anything else.

On the other hand she had been the one to fall in love with a shirt, I reminded myself; so she must have *something*.

'There is nothing here that I could wear to work,' she said. 'There is nothing here that I could wear at home. Family life. What's the point?'

'But it's *you*, that coat. You can see that,' I declared. 'Apotheosis clothes, that's what this place is for.'

You would never look at me and think, There goes a well-dressed woman. Outside work I do not dress to please anyone except myself. The concept of rational dress has always appealed strongly: useful pockets and plimsolls and William Morris' thoughts on vegetable dyes. If I want to look like a happy madwoman, I can. I'm paying for these clothes, I'm having fun. All this goes against the revered French approach: the top two buttons undone; the neat waist cinched; the short short skirt. The French wouldn't like this shop – it's too eccentric, there's too much colour. And as for that vile cynical Gallic maxim which holds that clothes should be chosen expressly *pour mettre en valeur* various good bits of the body! Leg or breast, sir? Bah, I say to this; *à bas les vêtements pimpants*; pimp clothes I call them. And for your information, no I am not fat. Nor am I thin. I'm just right.

Then Isobel caved in. Her defences crumbled, reason fled. She didn't care about the money any more, she stopped looking at the little tickets and their prices. Instead she narrowed her eyes and started to hunt down the most fantastical, the most artfully bizarre. I knew I hadn't been mistaken. I knew she had an eye. We were two of a kind when it came to this. She'd caught on. She was caught in. From now on she was a driven woman.

Soon we had amassed enough between us to start trying on. In the little side lavatory off the showroom – Wurstigkeit had nothing as utilitarian as a changing room – with silks and velvets over the rusted old wash basin, elbows in each other's faces, we struggled into mad dresses, lunatic ensembles. I barely knew this woman, I'd only met her once before, yet here we were taking off our clothes together in a rusty cubicle.

I tried on a cotton shirt first, raspberry-coloured and almost raspberry-scented as I pulled it over my head. I could smell the cleanness of the cotton, and the pleasant smell of our sweat, recent, slight and grassy, then wafting stronger from under our arms. Touching the cotton to my face, my cheek, I found it as fine as a baby's skin, and sighed.

She's much taller than me, Isobel. I'm not short, but my eyes were level with the great mamelonated nipples of pregnancy spread out by the gauze of her bra. I looked away. I hoped she wouldn't appraise what she saw of me with that merciless female regard which is so chilling. You must have seen the way women look at each other in dressing rooms or at the gym – furtive, assessing, without lust or kindness, hypercritically alert to any sign of age or deterioration. No wonder there is so little nakedness in British life. We live under a cloud inside our clothes, blue-veined as cheese, bluish-white as milk.

'I would love to hold a baby again,' I said, thinking back to that good dense beanbag weight.

'For half an hour,' she said shortly, struggling inside a hiss of silk. 'I'm not that keen on babies *per se*.' Her head surfaced above the glinting tussore and she scowled. She really did look impressive when she scowled, her features baroque and curly round the long straight nose.

'All those vile health visitors in hospital moralising about breast-feeding,' she shuddered.

It was on the tip of my tongue to mention antibodies, just for fun, but I thought she might punch me in the face.

When I had my daughter, I expressed my milk at home and at work; the freezer hoarded those precious cubes for the nanny to defrost; I carried the agonising breast pump round in my handbag as reverently as if it were a holy relic. The milk I managed to collect in the Ladies at work I stored at the back of the office fridge in a clearly-marked bottle until I could take it home. I stopped all that rather abruptly when my secretary one day came and whispered to me that there was a rumour that the boys in Sales were adding vodka. To the milk. Which is the sort of thing that seems mere infantile fun before you have a baby, but cruelty itself afterwards. I could see I might have seemed too earnest to them about the baby-feeding business. They simply couldn't begin to imagine. That was almost seven years ago, though.

'Have you got a good nanny?' I asked as I pulled on a stretchy velvet skirt like pliable moss.

'I loathe her with a passion,' she said, her voice muffled as she drew the dress back up. 'So do the children. But she's excellent, she runs the entire domestic show, I couldn't do without her. Anyway it's good for them to realise that life isn't just about what *they* want all the time. It's not a picnic.'

Whenever I ache for another baby, I think about the whole nanny business and think again. One child was fine. I mean, it was too much for my husband. In the year after she was born, he said he was wilting, he no longer felt free. (Do you know, that's exactly how *I* felt.) Then in the second year he said, 'I don't feel I can grow unless I leave,' and, dashing a manly tear from his eye, he left. I've kept the same nanny, for whom it is an ideal job. Nannies tend to jump ship at new babies, but I didn't rock the boat and now she's like my wife.

I looked at the glamorous velvet against my thighs, its pile as close as sheep-nibbled grass, soaking up light and sound.

'Wouldn't it be nice to be covered with this all over,' I said dreamily, 'Like a cat.'

'What,' she said, frowning. 'A catsuit?'

'What's a catsuit?'

For an instant I saw a cat unzip its fur and step out naked into the sun. I caught my eye in the mirror above the basin. Some days I look at my face – I might be a bit tired – and find myself thinking, That could do with a press with a damp cloth. Time marches on. Recently a graininess like slub silk has appeared in the valley between my breasts, where a few months ago all was perfectly

150

smooth and unmarked. It's more obvious after sleep, and rather fascinating to see age approaching in leaps and bounds. The man for whom I had not been able to spare the time was suddenly upon me, an excellent weight, for those few ideal moments when my knees had been drawn up into the made-to-measure hollows of his armpits.

'It's hot in here,' I said, and heaved another sigh.

In that cramped washroom space, trying not to catch each other's elbows or noses as we pulled garments over our heads, tugged others along our thighs, eyes averted, up in the air, musing apparently on other things, I caught glimpses of Isobel's baby-packed belly and of her extra-long limbs, more bone and health than is usually a woman's share, and wondered for a moment how she and her husband had sex together. Did she go up and catch him by the lapel like a judo wrestler? Did he rugby tackle her from behind and bring her down like that? Or did she collapse elegantly onto a chaise longue, a giraffe, a folding ruler, gradually succumbing? Perhaps there was no surrender; possibly she was proactive in her rapprochement with her husband, chucking him under the chin, bearhugging him, exchanging sportive punches. Hard to imagine how a very tall strong woman comports herself here. Shrinking and passivity would look ridiculous, like a mountain trying to be a mouse. You'd have to live up to your stature, be splendid, remote, brave, ungirlish. To be big and tall and spiritless would be worse than being little and short and spiritless; as somehow more of a waste, like an uninhabited tenement building. I reflected on the spite tall women endure, as though they're not entitled to that extra length of bone, as though there's something risible about it; and, frequently, their woundedness in the face of this, the

151

huddled quality which makes them the diametrical opposite of so many short men who go round causing trouble,
demanding more space and attention than they were born
with. Than their mothers could give them.

Anyway, there was nothing passive or spiritless about
Isobel. She was full of power. Back in the shop where we
went to stand in front of the long mirror, a sweet-faced
young salesgirl had attached herself to her splendour,
eyeing her with the shrewdness of a lover, pulling out this,
then this, then that for her to try. Despite herself, Isobel
was impressed.

'That on you,' I said excitedly of the strange item the girl
had persuaded Isobel to try, pelisse-like but sleeved, pink
and fawn and minutely pleated as the gills on the underside
of a field mushroom. 'That's so clever, like Mme de
Sevigné meets Simone de Beauvoir.'

'Hmmm,' she said, staring hard at herself in the mirror.

'I think it's right for you,' murmured the salesgirl.

She was some fifteen years younger than either of us, a
few inches of golden stomach open to the air, her navel
pierced with a diamond-tipped silver ring. Isobel and I are
both in our mid-thirties, the age of heroes in Russian
novels, halfway through the threescore years and ten.

'Try this,' said the girl to Isobel, holding against her a
dress in a green the violent colour of a cricket pitch before
a thunderstorm.

'Yes,' said Isobel slowly, nodding.

The girl dropped an acid-yellow mantilla over her left
shoulder and we let out our collective breath with a hiss.
She smiled in triumph.

After that, Isobel was in the buying vein. Straight on to
the yes pile went a jacket the good honest colour of carrots

and their paler core; a grey linen suit with the mauveness of dry earth; a blue-and-white dress like a willow-patterned teacup.

I cannot imagine what colour has to do with emotion, but the two are certainly inextricable. When I call my daughter to mind, I see her pale hot eyes, a furious light blue, fair-fringed, and the coral-freckled pink pallor of her father's thin skin. My best friend (to use my daughter's terminology) appears, and her celadon eyes are full of understanding without hardness, translucent, like sage backlit or the clear green of chives, their colour and light remarkable as if reflected off a silver plate.

When I think of women I know, I always see their eyes; with men, I see their mouths, their hands, the shape of their heads. I've tried to imagine why this is, and can only conclude that it's because women and men still do not fully meet each other's gaze.

Isobel's mobile phone sang out in muffled urgency from her bag. It was buried beneath a heap of bias-cut frangipani-petalled skirts and pinstriped peignoirs, pink plush toreador pants and a richly ribboned peajacket.

It rang and rang.

She looked at the heap of clothes as though it cradled a howling baby. She scowled, and the frown line between her brows was like a fault-line running clean through her.

'Leave it,' I said. 'I can't even hear it.'

'It might be important,' she said.

I shrugged.

It stopped after a while.

Both of us ought to have been somewhere else. Both of us had too much to do. Her time is so precious that it is charged out to other people at a pound a minute. Five pounds a minute. Ten!

I never have enough time. I work an eleven-hour day, excluding commuting. That means my nanny has to work a thirteen-hour day. I have to be out before seven in the morning, and if I'm lucky I'm back to kiss my daughter goodnight.

Isobel's words floated back to me from that high-flying *FT* interview. 'It's unreal to say you can balance work and children. At the end of the day you have to make up your mind whether you're going to bake cakes with them or go to work.'

Cakes again! Why do hard-working women always bring cakes into it when they're discussing childcare? Nobody bakes cakes these days, they're difficult to cook and bad for us. Surely we should be more concerned about the impossibility of persuading the childminder to prepare, and then to persuade the children to eat, plain fresh food. That's invisible work all right; *that's* a labour of love. But no, it's always cakes that are mentioned. It's obviously something to do with having our cake and eating it.

'Do you feel guilty?' I asked Isobel.

'What about?' she said.

'Work,' I mumbled. 'The children.'

'Why should I?' she said. 'If you don't want to be financially dependent on your partner, then you have to work. That's obvious.'

How strange, I thought; that sounds just like the sort of thing you say *before* you have children. And after all the what my ex-husband would term 'personal growth' I've been through in recent years, nothing is obvious to me any more.

'Anyway,' she continued, 'guilt is not a useful emotion.' I almost fell on the floor. I had never before considered emotion in terms of its usefulness. I was amazed.

'Try this,' said Isobel, surprising me again.

And so I tried on a long peculiar dress, yellow as a pear with mulberry-stained panels from armpit to hem, and a sash which tied over the stomach making a present of the wearer like the bow on a box of chocolates. It was a wild figment. It was unhinged. And yet I stood between big Isobel and the little salesgirl and we all smiled at the mirror, even Isobel, that expert shopping smile. The dress was made for me.

The salesgirl held up her fingertips in some cabalistic continental sign indicating perfection. I don't look at my reflection much these days, but now I was doing so and felt rather shy, like laughing, as though seeing a once-close friend after a long time. Isobel said. 'That's you. It's got that look you have. Don't mind me saying so.'

She was a little embarrassed. After all, we didn't know each other from Adam. These were intimate exchanges. And yet we probably saw the point of each other, the visual point, more than our husbands, or ex-husbands, did.

Do you know that old euphemism 'a bit of the other'? To me it suggests a different world just on the edge of our own, a middle-earth free of the usual cares and weights. Well, this dress was a bit of the other, it was what you might wear to a middle-earth party. I felt aerated and energised, the very opposite of the creeping dismay which descends when you buy and immediately know you should not have bought, so that the new garment dogs you grimly, haunts you miserably, to flap at you from the touchline of your dreams.

As for Isobel, she had accumulated a heap of finery and was now standing frowning by the till while they totted up how much it would cost. She looked like a baffled monarch, unable to believe that she was preparing to hand over vast sums to these illusionists.

'I think these things are right for you,' said the salesgirl consolingly. She smiled and nodded her head and wandered back to her patch.

We were now in the hands of two assiduous bustling boys. One was removing the price tags and the other was folding and wrapping.

'This gilet, it does not have a ticket,' said the first boy. ''Ow much is it?'

The second boy raised a quizzical eyebrow.

'One hundred fifty? Two hundred, I think.'

He shrugged, and held it in the air, hallooing up to his colleague in the chemise gallery.

''Ow much is this, Gianni?'

'Three hundred.'

'Three hundred,' he repeated, turning back, unblinking.

'Three unnerun *fifty*,' called someone from another corner of the shop.

Figures ricocheted around in the air, as at an auction.

'No, three hundred,' came the final estimate from the woman at the till, chimed out as though announcing a bargain.

Isobel moved her head from side to side as if she had been swimming and was trying to shake the water from her ears.

After such an exchange in Wurstigkeit, everything is so unreal that payment becomes something oddly casual and insouciant. You are anaesthetised against the usual anxiety at handing over money. It is pure thaumaturgy. I remembered my own first visit here, years ago, when I had asked the price of something, and politely scoffed at the answer and walked out. Then I'd walked around the narrow streets thinking about the silly little garment in question, and it was just like coming down with flu. Actual feverishness joined forces with a sense of suddenly lowered resistance and I had gone back in and handed over my money.

'You've got to hand it to them,' I quipped.

Isobel gave a wan smile.

'Let's see,' she said, 'I'd have to wear that dress eight hundred times before it came down to thirty pence a wearing. So that's twenty-seven times a year until I'm sixty-five.'

'You would spend the same on a picture,' commented the woman at the till. 'Is the same thing.'

'Is *not* the same thing,' hissed Isobel to me.

'Have them both,' I said, as she havered between two shirts, the one pale pink and the other bright Saxe blue.

'You've got to make choices, Laura,' she said sternly. 'You can't have everything.'

'Why not?' I enquired. 'Here at least.'

I wandered off while she paid. When I returned she sat sprawled on a chair, flushed and exhausted and leaden-eyed.

Our salesgirl approached with a little tray holding a crystal noggin of eau-de-vie and a few frail sugar biscuits. These Isobel wolfed down.

Then she said crossly, 'What are they *for*.'

We turned and watched as a pair of cowry-trimmed chaperejos was wrapped in silver tissue paper.

'They are smart but casual,' pronounced the beautiful boy who was wrapping them.

'Yeah yeah,' said Isobel rudely.

Back in her work clothes, the spell was wearing off. She glanced at her watch and clicked her tongue impatiently.

'You can wear them anywhere,' he insisted, looking up from under raven's wing brows.

'Like where?' snapped Isobel.

He shrugged superbly.

'You can do the gardening in them,' he said.

'Oh yes of *course*,' said Isobel. 'The gardening!'

And at last she capitulated. She was positively wreathed in smiles. I barely recognised her. Amusement played on her face and made it appear like floating quicksilver. She was transmogrified; she had literally lightened up.

'I can offer you a five per cent discount,' said the boy, superbly magnanimous.

'Well,' she gurgled, 'That might just tip me over the edge.'

I glanced at my watch. Good grief, was that the time? It was.

Things started to move fast. Her five per cent was restored in a hurry, the crackling carrier bags were handed across like hot cakes, and we were out in the real world again, turfed out onto the pavement with the numberless door closed firmly behind us.

'Where are you going next?' she asked.

'Eastcheap.'

'We can share a cab,' she said. 'Do you know, I've got eight hundred pages to read before four o'clock.'

We were walking fast towards the main road, almost skipping. Her strong face was alive with pleasure and sweetness, silvery and flickering with smiles like water in the sun.

'And I've got to go and interview the Head of Sales.' I laughed. 'Guilty as hell. Out on his ear!'

'That reminds me,' she said, slowing down for a moment. 'Now I've paid, I want the password.'

'Fair enough,' I said.

We stopped, she stooped down, and I stood on tiptoe to whisper it into her ear.

She laughed aloud.

Hurrah for the Hols

These were the dogdays all right, these last flyblown days of August. Her maternal goodwill was worn threadbare. This was the nadir of Dorrie's year, all this holiday flesh needing to be tended and shameless bad temper on display.

She was sitting at a table in the unshaded barbecue area by the pool over a cup of terrible coffee. And yet it was supposed to be the annual high-water mark, their summer fortnight, particularly this year when they had rejected camping or self-catering in favour of splashing out on a room in this value-for-money family hotel.

'You really are a stupid little boy. You're really pushing your luck,' said the man at the next table to one of the three children sitting with him. 'I want to see that burger finished *now*. Can't you for once in your whole life . . .'

His voice was quiet and venomous. What was he doing here alone with his children? It must be the same as Max was doing with their three now, playing crazy golf to give her some time to herself. This man's wife was probably just round the corner over just such another cup of coffee. Was she too feeling panic at not making good use of that dear-bought commodity, solitude?

'If you don't do what I say right now there'll be no ice cream. No swimming. No puppet show. I mean it.'

The small boy beside him started to cry into his burger, wailing and complaining that his teeth hurt.

'And don't think you're going to get round me like that,' snarled the man. 'I'm not your *mother*, remember!'

All over the place, if you listened, you could hear the steady exasperated undertone of the unglamorously leisure-clad parents teasing their tempestuous egomaniacal little people into, for example, eating that sandwich up 'or I tell you what, and you're being very silly, but you won't be going to the Treasure Island club tonight and *I mean it*.' It stuck in her throat, the bread of the weeping child. The parents said nothing to each other, except the names of sandwich fillings. She and Max were the same, they couldn't talk over, under or round the children and so it turned them sour and obdurate in each other's company. They held each other at night in bed but again could say or do nothing for fear of their children beside them, sleeping like larks, like clean-limbed breathing fruit.

She sipped and grimaced and watched the snail's progress of the combine harvester on the adjacent cliff. There was a splash as someone jumped into the pool, and a flapping over wasps and a dragging round of high chairs to plastic tables, and howls, hoots, groaning and broken-hearted sobbing, the steady cacophony which underscores family life en masse. At least sitting here alone she had been noticing the individual elements of the composition, she realised with surprise and some pleasure. When she was with her brood she noticed nothing of the outside world, they drank up all her powers of observation.

Here they came now, off the crazy golf course, tear-

161

stained, drooping, scowling. Here comes the big bore, and
here come the three little bores. Stifle your yawns. Smile.
On holiday Max became a confederate, saying things like
'They never stop' and 'That child is a cannibal.' Their
constant crystalline quacking, demanding a response,
returning indefatigable and gnat-like, drove him mad.
There must be something better than this squabbly nuclear
family unit, she thought, these awful hobbling five- and six-
legged races all around her.

She could see they were fighting. She saw Martin hit
Robin, and Robin clout him back. It was like being on
holiday with Punch and Judy – lots of biffing and shrieking
and fights over sausages. What a lumpen, moping, tearful,
spiritless mummy she had become, packing and unpacking
for everybody endlessly, sighing. Better sigh, though, than
do as she'd done earlier that day, on the beach when,
exasperated by their demands, on and on, all afternoon,
she'd stood up and held out her hands to them.

'Here, have some fingers,' she'd snarled, pretending to
snap them off one by one. 'Have a leg. Have an ear. Nice?'
And they had laughed uproariously, jumping on her and
pinning her to the rug, sawing at her limbs, tugging her
ears, uprooting her fingers and toes. Such a figure she cut
on the beach these days, slumped round-shouldered in the
middle of the family encampment of towels, impatience on
a monument growling at the sea. Or was it Mother
Courage of the sand dunes, the slack-muscled white body
hidden under various cover-ups, headgear, dark glasses,
crouched amidst the contents of her cart, the buckets, wasp
spray, suncream, foreign legion hats with neck-protective
flaps, plastic football, beach cricket kit, gaggle of plastic

jelly sandals, spare dry swimsuits, emergency pants. If she lumbered off for a paddle all hell broke loose.

'Did you have a nice time?' she said weakly as they reached her table.

Martin was shrieking about some injustice, his father's face was black as thunder. Robin sprinted to her lap, then Maxine and Martin jumped on her jealously, staking their claim like settlers in some virgin colony.

'She's not your long-lost uncle, your mother,' said Max, unable to get near her. 'You only saw her half an hour ago.'

Things got worse before they got better. There was a terrible scene later on. It was in the large room by the bar, the Family Room, where at six o'clock a holiday student surf fanatic led all the young children in a song and dance session while their parents sagged against the walls and watched.

> And a little bit of this
> And a little bit of that
> And shake your bum
> Just like your mum

sang the children, roaring with laughter as they mimed the actions. After this, glassy lollipops were handed out, and then the surfer started to organise a conga. The children lined up, each holding the waist of the one in front, many of them with the lollipops still in their mouths, sticks stuck outwards.

'That's dangerous,' mumured Dorrie. 'If they fell,' and she and other mothers discreetly coaxed the sweets from

163

the mouths of their nearest offspring with earnest promises that these would be returned immediately the dance had finished. Then she glanced across the room and saw Martin in the line, lollipop stick clamped between his teeth. Max just beyond him, sipping from his first bottle of beer, caught her eye; she, without thinking as hard as she might have done, indicated to him the lollipop peril, miming and pointing.

The conga had started, the music was blasting out, and yet when Max wrenched the stick from between Martin's clenched teeth the boy's screams were louder even than the very loudly amplified Birdy song. Martin broke out of the line and fought his father for the lollipop. Max, looking furious, teeth bared inside his dark beard, was a figure both ridiculous and distressing, like a giant Captain Haddock wrestling with an hysterical diminutive Tintin. Their battle carried on out in the hall, where Max dragged Martin just as the conga was weaving past, with screaming and shouting and terrible fury between them. They were hating each other.

Dorrie edged up to them, horror-struck, and the next thing was that Max was shouting at *her*. All right, it was their first day, they were all tired from the journey, but this was dreadful. The other parents, following the conga, filtered past interestedly watching this scene.

'Don't, don't, don't,' said Dorrie several times, but softly. The other two children joined them, sobbing.

At last she got them all past reception and up the stairs.

'I don't like you, Daddy,' wailed Martin through tears.

'I know you don't, Martin,' huffed Max, storming off ahead.

Really, he was very like Martin, or Martin was very like

him – both prone to explosions of aggressive self-defensive-ness – although of course Martin was six, whereas Max was forty. Because Max did this, she had to do the opposite in order to redress the balance, even though doing so made her look weak and ineffective. He sometimes pointed this out, her apparent ineffectiveness. But what would he rather? That she scream at them like a fishwife? Hit them? Vent her temper or ignore them, like a man? Let them get hurt? Let them eat rubbish? Let them watch junk? Just try doing it all the time before you criticise, not only for a few hours or days, she reflected, as she reined herself in and wiped tears from blubbing faces and assisted with the comprehensive nose-blowing that was needed in the wake of such a storm.

At least he didn't hit them when he lost his temper. She had a friend whose husband did, and then justified it with talk of them having to learn, which she, Dorrie, could not have borne. She really would much rather be on her own with them, it was much easier like that. Like a skilful stage manager she had learned how to create times of sweetness and light with the three of them; she could now coax and balance the various jostling elements into some sort of precarious harmony. It was an art, like feeding and building a good log fire, an achievement. Then in would Max clump, straightways seizing the bellows or the poker, and the whole lot would collapse in ruins.

'I'll get them to bed, Max,' she said. 'Why don't you go for a swim or something.'

'I'll wait for you in the bar,' he said frostily. 'Remember they stop serving dinner at eight.'

'Yes.'

'Don't forget to turn the listening service on.'

'No.'

'I know when I'm not wanted.'

She choked down her reply, and gently closed the door behind him.

'Now then,' she said, smiling at their doleful tear-smeared faces. 'What's up? You look as though you've swallowed a jellyfish!'

They looked at her, goggling with relief, and laughed uncertainly.

'*Two* jellyfish!' she said, with vaudeville mirth.

They laughed harder.

'And an *octopus*!' she added.

They fell on the floor, they were laughing so hard.

The second day was an improvement on the first, although, as Dorrie said to herself, that would not have been difficult. They turned away from the glare of the packed beach towards leafy broken shade, walking inland along a lane whose hedges were candy-striped with pink and white bindweed. A large dragonfly with marcasite body and pearlised wings appeared in the air before them and stopped them in their tracks. Then they struck off across a path through fields where sudden clouds of midges swept by without touching them. When they reached a stream overarched by hawthorn trees the children clamoured to take off their sandals and dip their feet in the water.

'This is the place for our picnic,' said Dorrie, who had brought supplies along in a rucksack, and now set about distributing sandwiches and fruit and bottles of water.

'We can't walk across the strand today,' said Max, consulting his copy of the Tide Tables as he munched away at a ham roll. 'Low tide was earlier this morning, then not again till nine tonight. Fat lot of good that is. But tomorrow looks possible.'

He had heard about an island not far from here which, once a day, for a short time only, became part of the mainland. When the tide was out you could walk across the strand to the island and visit the ancient cell of the hermit who had lived centuries before in the heart of its little woods.

'There doesn't seem to be any logic to it,' said Dorrie, looking over his shoulder at the week's chart. 'No pattern to the tides, no gradual waxing and waning as with the moon. I thought the tides were supposed to be governed by the moon, but they're all over the place.'

The children sat by them, each with a bag of crisps, nibbling away busily like rodents.

'There *is* a pattern, though,' said Max. 'When there's a new moon or an old moon, the tides are at their highest and also at their lowest. It's all very extreme at those times of the month, when the earth, moon and sun are directly in line.'

Martin, having finished his own bag of crisps, was now busily capturing ants from the grass and dropping them into his sister's bag.

'Don't do that,' said Dorrie.

'And when the moon's at right angles to the sun, that's when you get neap tides,' continued Max. 'Less extreme, less dramatic. What the hell's the matter *now*.'

Maxine had been trying to pull her bag of crisps away from Martin, who had suddenly let go, with the result that Maxine's crisps had flown into the air and over the grass,

167

where Martin was now rolling on them and crushing them into salty fragments.

'Stop it!' called Dorrie.

'Get up this minute!' shouted Max.

'Why should I, it's a free country,' gabbled Martin, rolling back and forth, enjoying the noise and drama.

'My crisps!' sobbed Maxine. 'They're all squashed!'

'What's your problem,' said Martin with spiteful pleasure, getting up as his father approached, and brushing yellow crumbs from his shorts. 'You threw them away, so that means you didn't want them.'

'I *didn't* throw them away!' screamed Maxine.

'Liar, I saw you,' goaded Martin. 'I saw you throw them in the air. Little liar.'

Maxine howled, scarlet in the face, struggling with her mother, who was trying to hold her, while Martin ran off out of range, dancing on the spot and fleering and taunting.

'Why is he such a poisonous little tick?' said Max, though without his usual fury.

On their way back to the hotel they passed a camp-site, and stopped by the gate to read its painted sign.

'Families and mixed couples only,' Maxine read aloud. 'What does that mean, Mum? What are mixed couples? Mum? Mum?'

'I'm not sure,' said Dorrie. She was reminded of her parents' description of looking for somewhere to rent when they first came to London, with the signs up in the windows reading 'No Blacks, No Irish' and her father with his Dublin accent having to keep quiet for a change and let her mother do the talking.

'Why do you suppose they want mixed couples only?' she murmured to Max. 'Why would they worry about gayness?'

'I don't think it's that,' said Max. 'I think it's more to put off the eighteen-thirty element; you know, bikers and boozers and gangs getting into fights.'

'You twenty years ago,' said Dorrie.

'Martin in ten years' time,' said Max.

'What's a couple?' persisted Maxine. 'What's a couple, Dad?'

'A couple here means a man and a woman,' said Max.

'Oo--a--ooh!' exclaimed Martin, giving Maxine a lewd nudge in the ribs and rolling his eyes.

'A husband and wife,' said Dorrie deflatingly.

'So a couple's like a family?' said Maxine.

'Yes,' said Dorrie.

'No,' said Max. 'A couple is *not* like a family. That's far too easy, just two people. It doesn't qualify.'

Dorrie was laughing now, and put her arms round his waist, her head in his shoulder. He kissed the top of her head and stroked her hair. The three children stood round looking at them with big smug smiles, beaming with satisfaction.

'Come in for a hug,' said Dorrie, holding out her arm to them, and they all five stood rocking by the side of the road locked into an untidy, squawking clump.

'You're looking well,' said Max, gazing at her that evening across the mackerel pâté and the bud vase holding the miniature yellow carnations. 'You've caught the sun. It suits you.'

'It was a good walk today,' said Dorrie, suddenly shy.

169

'They're lovely but they're very tiring,' said Max, draining his glass of beer. 'Exhausting. You should be more selfish.'

How can I, thought Dorrie, until you are less so? It's a seesaw. But she kept quiet. He went on to talk about the timberyard, how it was doing all right but they couldn't afford to rest on their laurels with all these small businesses going down all round them.

'We're a team,' declared Max, grandiose, pouring another glass for them both.

'Ye-es,' said Dorrie. 'But it's a bit unbalanced, don't you think, the teamwork, at the moment?'

'Are you saying I don't work hard enough?' demanded Max.

'Of course not,' said Dorrie. 'You work too hard. Don't be silly. No, I meant, you do all the work that gets somewhere and gives you something to show for the effort and pulls in money, but the work I do doesn't seem to get anywhere, it doesn't show, it somehow doesn't count even though it needs doing of course.'

'I don't see what you're driving at,' said Max, starting to look less cheerful.

'I don't know,' said Dorrie. 'At the moment I feel sub. Sub something.'

'Suburban?' suggested Max.

'Subordinate?' said Dorrie. 'No.'

'Submerged, then. How about submerged.'

'That's nearer. Still not quite . . . I know! Subdued. Though submerged is growing on me. Submerged is accurate too. That time at Marks, all my twenties, half my thirties, it's like a dream. I've almost forgotten what it used to be like.'

170

And she tried to explain to Max her feeling about this encroaching blandness, adaptability, passivity, the need for one of them at least to embrace these qualities, even if this made them shudder, if the family was going to work.

'We all have to knuckle down,' he said. 'Sooner or later.'

'It's just it seems, some of us more than others.'

'If we want to join in at all,' opined Max. 'Life. It's called growing up.'

'It doesn't feel like growing up,' she muttered from her side of the fence. Rather it felt like being freeze-dried and vacuum-packed. Knuckled down was putting it mildly.

'Well, as I said, whatever you're feeling like, you're looking well,' said Max; and that made them both feel better.

'Lovely, in fact,' he added, leaning across to touch her face meaningly.

After dinner, sitting in the Family Room drinking coffee, they found themselves drawn into a quiz game provided by the hotel as the adult equivalent of the children's conga. The quizmaster was a sparky woman in an emerald green jacket and pleats. She split them into groups and bossed them through an unnecessary microphone.

'What's the other name for kiwifruit?' she demanded, and echoes bounced off the ceiling. The groups whispered and giggled and scribbled on their scoresheets.

'What flag is all one colour?' she asked. 'Here's a clue, somewhere not very nice. Ooh, I hope no one from there is in this room!'

'Birmingham?' suggested Max.

'Very funny, the bearded gentleman,' said the woman. 'Now we're out of Miscellaneous and onto the Human

171

Body. Let's see how much you all know about the body, you jolly well should considering your age. And the one who's paying for the holiday will certainly be hoping to know a bit more about the human body of the opposite sex or else they'll have wasted their money, won't they?'

Dorrie's mouth fell open, she nearly dropped her drink, but nobody else batted an eyelid.

'And we've quite enough children here thank you very much while we're on the subject so let's hope you all know what you're up to,' continued the woman, arching a roguish eyebrow. 'Right. Now. Where are the cervical nerves?'

'And where's your sense of humour?' Max whispered into Dorrie's ear, observing her gape rudely at the woman.

In bed that night surrounded by their sleeping children, they held each other and started to kiss with increasing warmth. He grabbed shamelessly between her legs, her body answered with an enthusiastic twist, a backward arch, and soon he was inside her. There must be no noise, and she had pulled the sheet up to their necks. Within a couple of minutes they were both almost there, together, when there came a noise from Martin's bed.

'Mum,' he said sleepily, and flicked his lamp on. 'Mum, I'm thirsty.'

Max froze where he was and dropped his head and swore beneath his breath. Martin got out of bed and padded over towards them.

'Did you *hear* me, Mum?' he asked crossly. 'I want some water. *Now.*'

Dorrie was aware of her hot red face looking up from under Max's, and heard herself say, 'In a minute, dear. Go back to bed now, there's a good boy.' Martin paused to stare at them, then stumbled over back towards his bed.

'Do you think he's been traumatised?' she whispered to Max, mortified, cheated of the concentrated pleasure which had been seconds away, the achievement of it, the being made whole.

'Do I think *he's* been traumatised?' growled Max incredulously, rolling off her.

'Where's your sense of humour, then?' she murmured in his ear, but he pulled away and turned his back on her. She didn't blame him.

Their third day's adventure was planned by Max. They were going to cross the strand and explore the hermit's island. Today the tide was out at a reasonable time of the morning and the sun was up too. They stood and gazed across the shining sands at the exposed island, which was now, for an hour or so only, part of the mainland.

'It's further than I thought,' said Dorrie. 'It looks well over a mile. Maybe two.'

'Half a mile at most,' said Max heartily. 'Let's get going, remember we're racing the tide. Come on you lot, shoes and socks in the boot.'

'I think they should wear their plastic sandals,' said Dorrie. 'I can see stones. Weed.'

'Nonsense,' said Max. 'Lovely sand, skipping across the golden sand. Don't fuss, don't spoil it all with fussing.'

'Skippety skip,' sang Robin.

'I still think,' said Dorrie.

'Give us a break,' said Max.

'I'm not wearing my jellies,' said Martin. 'No way.'

'No way,' echoed Maxine.

When they started walking they were less downright, but by then it was too late. The gleaming silver-pink sand was knotted with wormcasts which made the children shudder, and studded with pebbles, and sharp-edged broken shells, which made them wince and squawk.

'Come on,' called Max, striding ahead on his prime-of-life leathery soles. 'We've got to keep moving if we're going to be there and back in time. Or we'll be cut off.'

Dorrie helped the children round the weeds, through ankle-deep seawater rivulets blue as the sky above, clucking, and lifting, and choking down irritation at the thought of the plastic sandals back in the boot.

'You were right, Mum,' groaned Martin mournfully. 'I wish I'd worn them.'

'So do I,' said Maxine, picking her way like a cross hen.

'So do I,' wept Robin, who was walking on tiptoe, as though that might spare his soft pink feet the wormcasts, and slowing them all down considerably.

'Come on,' yelled Max, a couple of hundred yards ahead.

'We can't,' yelled Dorrie, who was by now carrying Robin across her front.

It felt desperate, like the retreat from Moscow or something. Trust Max to engineer a stressful seaside event, trust Max to inject a penitential flavour into the day. They were by now half a mile out; it would be mad to go on and dismal to turn back. The sun was strong but muffled by haze, and the sky glared with the blanched fluorescence of a shaving light.

'What's all the fuss about?' said Max, having unwillingly rejoined them.

'I think we'll have to turn back,' said Dorrie. 'Look at

the time. Even if we make it to the island we won't be able to explore, we'll have to turn round and come straight back and even then we'd bc cutting it fine. Why don't you go alone, darling, you're quicker on your own.'

'You always have to spoil it, don't you?' said Max, furious as a child. 'You never want anything I plan to work.'

'Their feet hurt,' pleaded Dorrie. 'Don't let's quarrel in front of them.'

'Robin, you'll come with me, won't you?' said Max, squatting down beside his son. 'I'll give you a piggyback.'

'Max,' said Dorrie. 'It's nearly midday, it's not safe, why don't you go ahead with the camera and take photos so we'll all be able to see the hermit's house when the film's developed.'

'Robin?' said Max.

'I don't know what to choose,' said Robin, looking from his father to his mother and back again. He was out of his depth.

Dorrie felt anger bulge up as big as a whale surfacing, but breathed it down and said again, 'Take the camera, darling, that way we'll all see the secret island,' and hung the camera round his neck. She made herself kiss him on the cheek. He looked at her suspiciously. The children brightened. She forced herself to hug him. The children cheered.

'All right,' he said at last, and set off across the wet sand, running simple and free as a Red Indian.

'I didn't know what to say, Mum,' said Robin, spreading his hands helplessly. 'Daddy said go on go with me not Mummy. You said no. I felt splitted in half.'

175

'It's all right,' said Dorrie. 'Now everybody's happy. Look at that seagull.'

Above them, floating on a thermal, was a big, white, cruel-beaked bird. Seagulls were always larger than you expected, and had a chilly fierce look to them, without gaiety. She could barely speak for rage, but did not assign it much importance, so used was she by now to this business of ebb and flow. Who else, she wondered, could be living at such a pitch of passion as she in the midst of this crew; so uncontrolled, so undefended?

Having poked around the hermit's mossy cell and raced the tide back, white-toothed wavelets snapping at his heels, Max was in a good mood for the rest of the day, and they all benefited. He felt he had achieved something. He *had* achieved something. He had conquered the island, he had patterned it with his footprints, he had written his name on the sandy floor of the hermit's very cell with his big toe. Next week he would show them the photographs to prove it.

When the sun was low in the sky and the children were asleep, Max suggested to Dorrie that she should go for a walk on her own, just down to the beach below the hotel.

'It'll do you good,' he said.

He was going to sit by the bedroom's picture window in the half-dark with a beer, and would probably be able to make out her figure if the light didn't go too fast.

'Are you sure you'll be all right?' she said.

'Go on,' he snorted. 'Before I change my mind.'

She walked down barefoot through the hotel gardens, across trim tough seaside turf bordered by white-painted palisades and recently-watered fuchsia bushes. Then she turned on to the low cliff path which zigzagged down to the beach and felt the longer grass brush against her legs, spiky marram grass softly spangled in the dusk with pale flowers, sea pinks and thrift and white sea campion.

Robin had had trouble getting to sleep that evening. Stay here, he had demanded tearfully, his hand on her arm; don't go. I won't go, she had said; close your eyes. She had stroked his temple with the side of her little finger. Gradually he had allowed himself to be lowered down, a rung at a time, towards the dark surface of sleep. He had given a tiny groan as she moved to get up, but he was too far gone to climb back. She had sat by him for a little longer, creaking with fatigue, looking at his quiet face, his still hand on her arm, savouring the deep romance and boredom of it.

There were no buildings now between her and the beach except for this last snug cottage to her left shedding light from its windows. She paused to look up at it. It must surely house an ideal family, sheltered and enclosed but with a view of the bay too. The father was reading his children a story, perhaps, while the mother brushed their hair. Where did this cosy picture come from? Certainly not from her own childhood. She turned away and carried on down to the beach.

It was lovely to stand barefoot, bare-legged indeed, invisible in the deep dusk, a great generous moon in the sky and her feet at the edge of the Atlantic. She looked out over the broad bosom of the sea and it was like an old engraving, beautiful and melancholy, and the noise it made was a sighing, a rhythmic sighing.

As sailors' ghosts looked back on their drowned selves, dismantled, broken up, sighing like the sea for the collarbone lost somewhere around the equator, the meta-tarsals scattered across the Indian Ocean, so she wondered whether there could ever be a reassembly of such scattered drowned bodies, a watery *danse macabre* on the wreckers' rocks beneath a full moon. Was it possible to reclaim the scattered-to-the-winds self? She was less afraid of death, or understood it a shade more, purely through coming near it each time she had had a baby; but apart from that, this puzzle was to do with the loss of self that went with the process, or rather the awareness of her individuality as a troublesome excrescence, an obsoletism. What she wanted to know was, was this temporary, like National Service used to be, or was it for good?

She was filled with excitement at standing by the edge of the sea alone under the sky, so that she took great clear breaths of air and looked at the dimming horizon, opening her eyes wider as if that might help her to see more. It filled her with courage and made her want to sing, something Irish or Scottish, sad and wild and expressive of this, this wild salt air, out here, and of how it was thrilling, being alive and not dead.

When she turned back across the beach, away from the water, it was dark. The orange lights of the hotel up on the hill lengthened on the wet black sand like pillars of flame. She reached the edge of the beach, where it met the rocks and turf above, and started to climb back. A bat bounced silently past her ear as she crossed the little bridge over the stream, and then she felt the dust of the earth path beneath her feet again. As she walked on, hugging herself against the fresh chill of the dark, she looked at the cottages built on the hills around the bay, their windows yellow lozenges of enclosed warmth in the night.

178

Now she was walking back past the house she had envied on the way down, the house which was so secure and self-sufficient with its warm lit windows and snug family within. And from this house came the wailing of a child, a desolate hopeless noise. It was coming from this very house. On and on it went, the wailing, steady and miserable, following her up the path. Her throat tightened and her eyes prickled, she called herself every sort of fool as she trudged on; and she physically ached to pick up and hold the weeping child, and tell it there there, there there, then smooth it down and stroke its hand until it slept. The comfortless noise continued, not a baby's crying but the sobbing of a child. No child should be left to cry like that, she thought, ambushed by pity, by memory; and − in a rage − people aren't bloody well nice enough to their children!

Don't be so soft, came the advice; crying never did any harm, you can't allow them to run the show or where will that land you? Let them take themselves to hell, those hard hearts who leave their children to cry themselves to sleep alone, and in hell they will have to listen to the sound of a child crying and know that they can never comfort it. That was what Dorrie was thinking as she climbed back up the hill.